THE
LAWGIVER

Center Point
Large Print

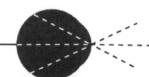

**This Large Print Book carries the
Seal of Approval of N.A.V.H.**

THE LAWGIVER

Herman Wouk

CENTER POINT LARGE PRINT
THORNDIKE, MAINE

This Center Point Large Print edition is published
in the year 2013 by arrangement with
Simon & Schuster, Inc.

Page 96: *Moses Breaking the Tablets of the Law*,
by Gustave Doré (1832–83) / Ken Welsh /
The Bridgeman Art Library

The text of this Large Print edition is unabridged.
In other aspects, this book may
vary from the original edition.
Printed in the United States of America
on permanent paper.
Set in 16-point Times New Roman type.

ISBN: 978-1-61173-649-6

Library of Congress Cataloging-in-Publication Data
Wouk, Herman, 1915–
The lawgiver / Herman Wouk. — Center Point Large Print edition.
pages cm
ISBN 978-1-61173-649-6 (library binding : alk. paper)
1. Moses (Biblical leader)—Fiction.
    2. Wouk, Herman, 1915– —Fiction
    3. Fiction—Authorship—Fiction.
    4. Motion pictures—Production and direction—Fiction.
    5. Hollywood (Los Angeles, Calif.)—Fiction. I. Title.
PS3545.O98L39 2013
813′54—dc23
                                                    2012041312

THE
LAWGIVER

A scuffed file in my desk drawer labeled *The Lawgiver* contains a few typed yellow pages turning brown with age. When I was writing *The Caine Mutiny*, it occurred to me that there was no greater theme for a novel, if I could rise to it, than the life of Moses. The file dates to that time. The years have rolled over me. I have not quailed at large tasks. World War Two and the wars of Israel were sizable challenges, but I took them on. *The Lawgiver* remains unwritten. I have never found the way to do it. Other ideas for books I have set aside (no time, no time!), but I still hope against hope for a bolt of lightning, which will yet inspire me to pen my own picture of *Maysheh Rabbenu*, the Rav of mankind.

—*From* The Will to Live On,
published May 2000

Chapter One

MR. GLUCK

BSW Literary Agency

HW:

Sorry to trouble you. That Andrea with the British accent just rang yet again. She already rang at 9 this morning on the dot. She said Mr. Warshaw would make it worth my while if I would put him through to Mr. Wouk on the phone even for a minute or two, "by mistake." (A gross offer of a bribe?) She still won't say what it's about.

OK, Ignore.

I ignored 3 calls from her yesterday and 2 on Friday. This will just go on and on.

Endure, and let me alone!

(Secretary on speakerphone) Look, HW, Tim Warshaw got through to me, told me what he wants to say to you, and asks for a couple of minutes, no more. I can't take the responsibility to pass this up. I told him I'd have to stay on the line and take notes. He laughed and said, "Why not?" Here he is.

WARSHAW: *(slow, deep voice)* Mr. Wouk?
HW: Yes.
WARSHAW: Sir, would one million dollars for a half-hour conference interest you?

(Insert by HW: A jolt. These Hollywood hoodlums! He has the money, he's riding high, Best Picture Oscar for his art-house breakout from the big disaster films. A million! . . . Family foundation, charities . . . son's divorce . . .)

HW: Mr. Warshaw, I'm ninety-six years old, trying to get one more book done while I last. Thank you, but—
WARSHAW: Sir, dare I ask what the new book is about?
HW: No.
WARSHAW: May I tell you what I'm calling about, and I swear that'll be that? I'll thank you and hang up—

HW: Go ahead.

WARSHAW: *(pause—slow, deep)* Moses . . .

HW: Moses?

WARSHAW: Moses, sir. Pharaoh, Burning Bush, splitting the sea—

HW: Oh, yes, that Moses. The one Cecil B. DeMille did twice—

WARSHAW: Sir, this would be all different. Think twenty-first century, think special effects—think maybe three-D—

HW: Mr. Warshaw, I've appreciated your approach. Most of all, your offer to thank me and hang up.

WARSHAW: Thank you, sir. I'm hanging up.

(He hangs up.)

9:10 a.m.

Blasted day yesterday, when I was just getting a handle on the new approach to this confounded book, or thought I was. Timothy Warshaw, the red-hot moviemaker of the hour, with an artsy departure from his disaster blockbusters—he copped an Oscar for Best Picture, *Midsummer Night's Dream*, directed by a nutty Japanese with a cast of all unknown teenagers in masks—the critics rolled over neighing and kicking their hooves in the air—this Warshaw phoned and offered me "one million dollars for a half-hour conference." Turned him down rudely. Last night at dinner we talked about it.

BSW: Good. That half-hour conference is baloney. He'd get his money's worth out of your hide, one way or another. Is this new "impossible novel" of yours really started?

HW: Two preliminary journal files. No copy yet. I was drafting the first page of an opening scene when Warshaw bulldozed past Priscilla and got to me.

BSW: What do you want to do about it?

HW: Nothing. Write the book.

BSW: Well, I've had my doubts, you know. Not much interest in Moses nowadays.

HW: Oh, no? What do you suppose Warshaw wanted to talk to me about? *(Imitates Warshaw.)* MO . . . SES . . .

BSW: No! Wow.

HW: Coincidence? What else? Security breach? Nobody, but *nobody,* except you—and Priscilla, typing my notes, and she's a silent tomb—knows that I've been working on a Moses novel.

BSW: It's a ploy.

HW: Forget it, then.

BSW: No. Give him the half hour, but don't take his money. Just listen.

HW: What's the point?

BSW: I'm curious. He'll spill something.

HW: You sit in.

BSW: Sure.

WARSHAWORKS
Century City, California 90067

From: Tim Warshaw
To: Hezzie Jacobs
          Nullarbor Petroleum, Houston
Subject: Wouk

Well, Hezzie, I did manage to get through to Wouk. You can tell this mysterious Australian investor of yours that it wasn't easy, and he wasn't encouraging. Wouk doesn't sound over the phone nearly as old as he is, going on 97, but he was abrupt and peevish. No interest whatever.

Surely if this investor is at all serious, his proposal can't hang on getting that mulish ancient to write the film. That's an irresponsible whim. It won't work. It's a deal breaker up front. Otherwise his offer is certainly intriguing and exciting. Why can't you put me in direct touch with him? An e-mail address, if not a phone number? I have persuasive power, you know. I got the bank to fund Yoshimoto's *Dream*, when you and other investors ran for the tall grass, telling me such dizzy nonsense hadn't a prayer. I'm looking at my Oscar on the desk as I write.

Tim

From the desk of

TIM WARSHAW

Andrea, hold everything. Call Hezzie Jacobs in Houston, tell him Wouk just phoned me. I'm off to Palm Springs in the Falcon. Order a limo to meet me Signature Airport. T.

4 p.m.

Another day shot, no new writing, no nothing. Warshaw's half hour—and he stuck to it, I'll say that—killed the day. Waiting for him to get here, settling him in for the half-hour conference, seeing him out the door, then chewing over this strange business with my lady, and here I am with one day less in my life to do what haunts me, "the impossible novel."

Here's Warshaw's pitch in brief. An Australian eccentric of great wealth wants a movie made about Moses, and is ready to fund it. The approach came via one Hezzie Jacobs, a Texas venture capitalist who sometimes dabbles in films, though his main interest is oil from algae. Jacobs has a vast project of algae ponds going in Nullarbor, Australia. This eccentric investor, a uranium tycoon, has money in it. When Jacobs told him a Moses film might cost two hundred million, all he said was, "Fair dinkum," Australian slang for *okay,* or the equivalent.

Now, here's what Warshaw left out, and it's crucial. My accountant, who's wired to insiders in the film game, tells me Warshaw in fact is over a barrel. The Oscar went to his head, he's always been a high flier, cross-collateralized up to his ears. He's put some new projects into develop-ment, and another of his disaster productions is getting filmed in Turkey right now, *Aeneas and Dido*, a sexy epic based on the *Aeneid*, with a fall of Troy bigger than D-day in *Saving Private Ryan*. He's been close to freezing that production, short of cash and low on credit, so the rumors fly. Still, he's meeting his huge budgets week by week and acting carefree as a hummingbird. And the back story on *that* (my accountant again, and this gets convoluted) is that Jacobs, knowing Fair Dinkum's obsession to get a Moses film made, has started quietly bankrolling Warshaw, gambling that sooner or later it'll happen, Fair Dinkum will come across with an investment of four or five hundred million dollars in WarshaWorks, and Jacobs figures to skim off lots of cream.

What it seems to come down to—and I begin to see why Warshaw was ready to pay me a million for a conference—is this: the uranium nabob either backs WarshaWorks with a whopper of a "stimulus" or Warshaw is in real trouble, and that seems to depend on whether he can get me to write a Moses film! So the thing stands. Distracting, but diverting, I have to say. Meantime, no work.

From: Rabbi Mordechai Heber

To: Mr. Herman Wouk

Subject: Hezzie Jacobs

Sorry to bother you, Mr. Wouk. A venture capitalist who owns a winter home here wants to see you. Mr. Jacobs is a good man, not religious, but he's kept my little day school alive. You know how I guard your privacy, but as a special favor to the children of our school, will you see him if he flies here tomorrow? I need an answer right away.

9 a.m.

The plot thickens. Exponentially. Not for my book, my third false start goes into the files, hopelessly wrong. It's the Fair Dinkum thing. Turns out that this Hezzie Jacobs owns a home here and is coming from Houston to talk to me. Rabbi Heber interceded for him. I don't say no to the rabbi . . .

NULLARBOR PETROLEUM LLC
"Freedom from Mideast Oil Through Algae"
HOUSTON—MELBOURNE

FAX (*STRICKLY CONFIDENTIAL*)

From: Hezzie Jacobs
To: Louis Gluck
Subject: Algae, Air Force, Moses, etc.

   Lou, good news about Wouk and Moses! A Palm Springs rabbi got me in to see him, and I told him all about you. I took a big chance, Louie. I told him that you'd fly from Australia to talk to him. You can always say I'm crazy, or your doctors won't allow you, but depending on how keen you are on the Moses film—which I still don't understand, but it's your time and money —this is your opening.

   Now, Lou, the big news is that the air force is sky-high on the algae! Those Arizona people put on a great show for the generals, took them around the ponds, had a Nobel Prize molecular biologist there, talking plain English about algae molecules and all that. The main thing was the green gasoline! It even smells different, kind of pleasant. They filled the tank of a jeep with it and went roaring down a highway and back, & those stiff generals with all their medals were joking and laughing, and they had a great buffet lunch with fine wine, and in short, the air force is interested, though at the moment that tankful of algae gasoline figures out at $54,000 a gallon. Louis, this can be the breakthrough. Yes, right now oil prices are down again, which is bad for algae, but looking ahead the world's oil is running out, no doubt of it. Now is the time for Nullarbor! Of the fifty-odd start-up companies doing algae, Arizgrene is the slickest, they know how to promote, but that's all. About Nullarbor's genetically altered molecule they haven't a clue.

This thing is starting to snowball, Louis, don't let it roll away from us! Where's your comment on the new prospectus?

Hezzie

Meeting with Louis Gluck

I've never felt the need of a tape recorder until now. In former days when I was badgered into an interview, I never allowed a tape recorder, maybe Gluck wouldn't have, either. Anyhow, here goes to bang out my recollections of the long, bizarre meeting while they're fresh and copious.

Mr. Gluck is something else. Uninvited, he flew here from Australia to see me. Hezzie Jacobs called me up out of the blue, said Fair Dinkum was at the Beverly Hills Hotel, and would come down to Palm Springs before flying on to Toronto, and from there to Paris, then to Beijing, and so back to Australia. Jacobs said he's done this globe circling for years. This is his second time this year, in February he went the other way from Melbourne via Mumbai, Capetown, Rio de Janeiro, Quito, and home. So Jacobs says, and I can believe it.

Whatever happens, I don't think I'll forget my first sight of Gluck, rolling through the door in a wheelchair, with one leg propped up on a board and a dark-skinned fellow pushing him. "Louie Gluck," he said holding out a hand. "You're going to write *The Lawgiver.* There's nobody else. This is Ishmael." The companion grinned and rolled him into the living room. Gluck's an old, old gent, round face, thin white hair, sharp blue eyes, voice hoarse but clear, piquant Jewish-Aussie accent. "Jacobs told me that you turned down Warshaw's million dollars and gave him half an hour for free. Smart, *smart*." I said that that was my wife's idea. "I want to meet her." I explained that I was trying to write a Moses book, and he should forget about involving me in a movie.

"You're making a big mistake. Nobody reads books, everybody watches movies."

"People read my books."

"I've read them all. That's how I know you'll write the *Lawgiver* movie. I'm talking volume. Take your *Winds of War*, for one person who read the book how many people saw the miniseries movie, all over the world? A million to one? Or counting all the Chinese who watched pirated copies of the miniseries—like the pile I saw in a Beijing supermarket—three million to one? Why are you trying to write a Moses book at your age?"

"Because I want to, and can afford to take the time, and I don't have that much time."

"Who knows how much time you've got, and why waste it? You want to say something worthwhile about Moses, something people will take away with them . . . Where can Ishmael get something to eat while we talk?" I sent Ishmael off to Sherman's Deli. "He's an aborigine," Gluck said. "Smart, *smart.* So, you want to write a book about Moses. You can do it, because you understand Moses, but you're wasting the time you've got, because—"

He was getting under my skin. *"Nobody* understands Moses," I barked at him. His face only lit up and he reached to shake my hand. Bony claw like mine. "See? I'm right. You're the man for the movie. Who else understands that nobody understands Moses? So let me ask you, why try to write about him altogether?"

Well, that triggered, against my better judgment, my song and dance about Moses as Atlas— Western world resting on his shoulders, Christianity and Islam meaningless without him, Lawgiver of the Christian Bible, "Divine Teacher" of the Koran, etc., etc. Gluck listened with a hungry look, nodding and nodding, and broke in as I was citing a Koran passage about Pharaoh, "All right, all right, I take your point, I'm a reasonable man. The few people who read books are important to you. So write your book *and* the movie, what's wrong with that? One day the screenplay, next day the book, next day the screenplay, and so on. Isn't that a good plan?"

"Mr. Gluck, I *can't* write a movie. I don't know how."

"You wrote those two miniseries."

"To protect the history, yes, just doing what the director told me. Anyway, it was another era. *Winds* ran eighteen hours, *Remembrance* thirty hours—"

He shifted ground. Yes, yes, he could see I was making sense, he was new in all this. Warshaw would get a younger writer, best in the business, money no object, the writer would consult me, and I'd have approval of every page he wrote. How about that? I told him wearily that the director creates the film, not the writer, and Spielberg was his man, a great writer-director, a giant of the film industry, a good Jew—

"Oh? So why did he make *Schindler's List* about a goy?"

Now he had me defending Steven Spielberg. "You missed the whole point. Because Schindler *wasn't* a Jew, the world audience could identify with him and enjoy a big Holocaust movie—"

"Why was *Munich* all about how wrong the Mossad was to hunt down the terrorists who killed the Israeli athletes? Did *you* feel sorry for those terrorists? Well, never mind, never mind, he's a good man, he does good things, he should live to be a hundred and twenty, making his fine movies, but you'll do *The Lawgiver*. We'll find a writer-director you approve of, and he'll get your approval on every scene. Let's settle on that—"

Ishmael returned at this point, full of praise for Sherman's pastrami, and reminded Gluck that his connection to Toronto was due at the airport in half an hour.

26

"No good. Get us on the next flight."

"Louie, we'll miss the plane to Paris."

"Phone Smodar, tell her to reschedule all the flights, I have to talk more with Mr. Wouk—" Aside to me, "My Gulfstream is down, I have to get to Beijing Tuesday—"

"Smodar, sir? It's three a.m. in Melbourne, what can she do?"

"The Qantas line's open all night—"

I had to put an end to this. I swiveled around and batted off as fast as I could type:

Dear Mr. Warshaw:

Mr. Louis Gluck is here in my office. If you find a writer-director who I believe can make a Moses movie measuring up to the subject, I'll consider acting as a consultant. Frankly, I see no possibility that you can come up with such a person. Even if you do, or at least think you do, I'm not bound by this note at all, except to consider your choice.

Herman Wouk

I signed and handed the printout to Gluck. "Here," I said. "Don't miss your plane." A quick businesslike glance, a nod, he asked for two more printouts, got me to sign them both, and I saw him out to the limousine. This Ishmael folded up the wheelchair and board and slid Gluck into the limo smooth as glass. That's how it went. BSW thinks I was an idiot to give him the note, says I'm in for a siege of nagging by Warshaw and pointless talks with writer-directors. Maybe. I *had* to get that Gluck out of my office, off my back.

NULLARBOR PETROLEUM LLC
"Freedom from Mideast Oil Through Algae"
HOUSTON—MELBOURNE

FAX (*STRICKLY CONFIDENTIAL*)

From: Hezzie Jacobs
To: Timothy Warshaw
                Cedars-Sinai Hospital
Subject: Lawgiver

Sorry about your ulcer, Tim. It's a wonder these past weeks haven't put you in Forest Lawn. You're an iron man and you'll soon be fine. This is urgent, or I'd let you alone. Gluck is cooling off, Tim. Not about the Moses film, about you and WarshaWorks. Lou is a nice guy, but peremptory. He doesn't understand the writer-director problem that's stymied you for so long, isn't interested, and is asking me about other studios.

What do you know about Margolit Solovei, a young writer-director? Wikipedia calls her a "phenom," a film business term for a fast starter, at 26 she's made three art-house movies and had a play on Broadway. Her brother and Rabbi Heber were yeshiva buddies, as it happens. She's the black sheep of the Solovei family, disappeared into showbiz, never mentions her deep Jewish background. Once when the rabbi and I were discussing Hollywood Jews, he cited her as a sad example. Why not consider Solovei? At least she's knowledgeable, and might conceivably hit it off with Wouk. A desperate long shot, but what's to lose, with Gluck getting damned impatient?

Hezzie

MARGO

Mommy dear,

Something has come up that you must tell Tatti. Not that it will change his mind about me. Just to show him that I'm not quite a lost soul, not altogether a worthless <u>schmata</u>. I'm going to Palm Springs tomorrow to confer about a Moses film with guess who, Herman Wouk. Tatti's never read a novel in his life, and never will, but he did read a God book Wouk wrote back in the '50s—I remember that because I got it for him from the library, though I needed another card after he tore up my first two. I'll write you again after I meet the author. I didn't know he was alive.

Your loving daughter,

Mashie

MARGOLIT SOLOVEI ENTERPRISES LLC
10235 SUNSET BOULEVARD
LOS ANGELES, CA 90077

Mr. Joshua Lewin
Lewin, Rubinstein & Curtis
1440 K Street, NW
Washington, DC 20005

Dear Joshua,

I received your semiannual letter, and to be honest I had no idea Rosh Hashanah was so close, I'm very busy and of course it means nothing to me, I haven't seen the inside of a shul in a dog's age. Sorry for this belated response, thanks anyway for your New Year wishes. Your letters are very touching, but disturbing as the years pass. It was all very well for you to say when we broke up that you'd wait for me until you die, but isn't it getting a bit silly? You can have your pick of a thousand religious Jewish girls, from the prettiest young ones to the few leftovers of my time. With your international law practice and your deep learning, you're as big a fish as was ever reeled in by a nice Jewish girl.

I'll reply to your letter more at length when I return from a meeting with Herman Wouk—yes, your favorite—to explore writing a Moses film. A major producer wants me to consider it, but it seems to be up to Mr. Wouk, I don't know why. So much for your gentle semiannual hints that I'm wasting my life out here, writing and producing ephemera while my biological clock ticks off the years unheard.

As ever,

Margo

Chapter Two
MARGO

For this interview I did obtain a tape recorder, and did some rehearsing with BSW, talking back and forth for voice levels, sound settings, etc. Solovei arrived around noon and left at three, declining lunch. Very pretty, all business. After polite chitchat with BSW in the living room I brought her into my office and turned on the recorder. My words are in italics.

Mr. Wouk, let me say at the outset that a Moses film is almost impossible, and even if it gets made it's a bad idea and will die at the box office. What we should do is a remake of *Marjorie Morningstar.* I've got my own company. That Marjorie movie they made in the fifties is a forgotten clunker. A two-hour film could be funny, pathetic, the love story's universal—
Why are you here? Moses doesn't interest you?
Well, actually, I spent the week you were in Tahoe rereading the Torah and—
King James version?
No, no, the *Humesh*, the Hebrew, I grew up on it. The story is gorgeous, monumental, I haven't

34

thought about it in years, but Moses, what a character! Growing up in Pharaoh's palace but never forgetting who he was—that was the mother's doing, of course, she and his siblings, Aaron and Miriam. By the time she brought him to the princess he was already an unchangeable Jew—growing up in the palace, the princess's pet Hebrew boy, lad grows to young man, kills the Egyptian taskmaster, flees to Midian, and lo, a *fifty-year* time lapse to the Burning Bush! Whereupon—

One moment, Margolit—

Margo. Margolit is my trade name, my real name, all right, friends call me Margo—

Margo, I didn't expect our talk to take this turn. Go on about Moses—fifty-year lapse— Burning Bush—

Oh, Lord, shall I? Well, then two years of the hard action of course, the DeMille stuff—ten plagues, splitting the sea, Ten Commandments, Golden Calf orgy, smashing the Tablets. Then the Spies, which DeMille skipped—and he was out of his mind, they're the pivot of the whole plot— then another huge time lapse, *forty* years, and they're at the Jordan River, Aaron dies and Moses can't enter the Holy Land, so he reviews the Laws for the new Israeli generation, climbs Mount Nebo, glimpses the Land, and dies. You've got two *Lawrence of Arabia*s in length and a hero nobody can write. He's at once holy and pathetically human and yet formidable as Caesar, it's all right there in the narrative, but you can't leave out much and make any truthful sense—

All right, Margo, enough! Tell me a little about yourself—

About my films?

No, I've seen them. Your background. A Hollywood writer-director who can read the Torah at sight?

Mr. Wouk, my father's a rabbi, a Bobover Hasid with his own small shul in Passaic, constant struggle to keep our big family fed, and strict? Even my long-suffering mother thinks he's over the top, and she stems from a big Satmar family, the Gronskis. Bless me, I haven't talked about this in I don't know how long. *Years!* Well, I freed myself from all that, obviously, went to Barnard, one thing led to another, and here I am, not too sure of what I'm doing in your office. My agent told me something about a uranium mogul in Australia who wants a Moses film made. WarshaWorks is involved, and you seem to be, too. Kind of confusing.

(At this point I filled her in on Louis Gluck, made her laugh, then she sobered.)

Why are you taking on such a responsibility?

I'm not taking it on. That uranium tycoon's a strong presence, that's all. So back to you. Quite a huge leap from Barnard to my office—

(Long pause, buzzing of the recorder.)

I'd have to disclose a dark secret I'm ashamed of.

Your choice.

(Another pause.)

No, I'm here for a job. You're entitled to ask. Arnold Granit—you've heard of him? Producer at Universal?

No.

Very big in the industry. Arnold Granit discovered me. I wrote plays at Barnard and, after that, finally got one produced off-off-Broadway. Ran two weeks. You couldn't have seen it. *Bobover, Bobover* I called it, a scurrilous send-up of my father. Granit by chance caught it, and the next day he phoned and took me to lunch at the Four Seasons. He bawled me out for *Bobover, Bobover*, said he laughed his head off and hated it, his own grandfather was a Satmarer. They're a lot stricter than Bobovers. "You're funny," he said. "We'll see what you can do with film comedy. Just don't touch Jewish material ever ever again, not for me—leave that stuff to the Mel Brookses and Woody Allens, understand?" Well, did *that* ever get my hackles up! I started to argue that such comedy of alienation was legitimate and important. He cut me short. "Sure, sure, only *not on my dime,* understand? There's a lot of Holocaust survivors out there, my grandfather's one . . ." Now, Mr. Wouk, can I ask you a question or two?

Shoot.

This uranium fellow—according to my agent, he wants you approving everything, the script, the cast, everything.

That's right.

Then I'm out. That's intolerable. There's raucous comedy in a *Lawgiver* movie, as well as a reach for the ineffable. Which has to fall short, but I'd have to try to do the thing my way—

Though not believing in any of it?

That's my private business, isn't it? The thing *can* be done, if Mr. Uranium will come up with the budget. Why me, is a question for you, and I'm not committing myself either—I came to find out what this is all about.

And did you?

Sort of. Needs digesting. *(Laughs.)* Frankly, it's freaky.

Talk about freaky, Margo, I've found out quite a bit, too.

(We both laugh. End of tape.)

WARSHAWORKS

FAX

From: Tim Warshaw
To: Hezzie Jacobs

(Dictated from my hospital bed.)

A ten-strike, Hezzie, thanks and congratulations! Wouk likes Margo Solovei! I've been trying and trying, flat on my back as I am, to contact Gluck. He's disappeared off the planet, or decided against the whole thing, or I don't know what, but phone calls, faxes, e-mails, BlackBerrys, nothing gets through to him. Hezzie, *get to Gluck!* There's been a quick development. Wouk's wife, also his agent, is considered in this town a madwoman, impossible to deal with, but smart. She's been against this whole thing, gave him holy hell about that note he handed Gluck. Now she wants to put the responsibility back on Gluck once and for all, so hubby can go back to his precious novel.

She's offering a get-together at her home, where Gluck can casually encounter Margo. If he likes her enough to go ahead, we're home. Margo won't accept Wouk breathing down her neck, some less restrictive arrangement will have to be worked out, but with the Gluck money assured I'll go ahead full steam, you'll recoup your advances with interest as agreed, and a new ball game starts.

Get to Gluck, and let me know!

Tim

NULLARBOR PETROLEUM LLC
"Freedom from Mideast Oil Through Algae"
HOUSTON—MELBOURNE

FAX

From: Hezzie Jacobs
To: Tim Warshaw
Subject: Gluck's whereabouts

Louie's off around the world again. Smodar, his secretary, an Israeli, is sweet as honey but hard as nails, I can get nothing more out of her. Couple of weeks ago he did gripe to me about his rubber plantations in Vietnam—seems rubber's a glut on the market right now and his local contractors are pulling up the trees and planting pepper trees. I checked with guys in Ho Chi Minh City who know Gluck. He was through there last week all right, but they don't know where he went next. He's traveling west, so he'll be passing through California going home, and maybe you can organize that Wouk meeting. You'd better! Sorry, Tim, I'm almost at the end of my goddamn rope with the Moses lunacy, I assure you. Unless Gluck comes through with the Warshaw financing soon, I'll have to pull out and write off my losses in this venture. My algae ponds are my future.

HJ

MARGOLIT SOLOVEI ENTERPRISES LLC
10235 SUNSET BOULEVARD
LOS ANGELES, CA 90077

Dearest Josh:

I've never asked you to do anything for me before. I've never before felt driven to do so.

Wouk hasn't rejected me out of hand for the Moses project! That's all I know, and I'm not even sure of that. Three other writer-directors with more and better credits got turned down fast. The producer Tim Warshaw called me today from his hospital bed, to ask me to hold off future commitments. Nothing more.

I *hate* to call my agent and crawl for news. I acted pretty high and mighty with Wouk, but the truth is I'd *kill* to do this Moses film. I can't sleep nights picturing this job. I see whole scenes, whole sequences, it's a skyscraping project, and nothing like it has ever been done, the

DeMille films were foolishness. I was *born* to do this, and I can do it precisely because I thought the whole religion through when I broke away. It takes someone who *knows*—not *believes*—to capture and picture the storytelling truth about Moishe Rabenu in a film. It may prove a dog at the box office, then again it may just work—but if this lunatic Australian will come up with the budget, what else matters?

Call me anytime, day or night, if you find out something. I'll be awake.

And thanks!

Mashie

From: Joshua Lewin
To: Margolit Solovei
Subject: Mrs. Wouk meeting

Sheldon Rubinstein, our firm's litigation man, has deep contacts in Hollywood. Sheldon reports that you'll meet the uranium gentleman at Wouk's home next Thursday, for dinner. Mrs. Wouk will invite you. Good luck, and love.

J.

12:30 a.m. Way past my bedtime. Unavoidable. *Never again.* Beer, I mean. The curry was pretty hot and the party was dying as BSW and I waited with Margo and Hezzie for Gluck to show up, so BSW suggested we start eating, and I had two beers, and I write this in a dizzy fog. How the mighty have fallen, I who once would slug down bourbon at night like black coffee to keep working—

He came blowing in very late. Literally! It was windy outside but not like in the northern part of town, his limo ran into a sandstorm and had to pull over. The meeting was inconclusive, perhaps a flop, and the whole nutty interlude is over, and maybe WarshaWorks goes bust, and I'm out from under. When I saw Gluck and Solovei sitting together with plates of curry on their laps and laughing, I thought there might be something doing, so I went and joined them. Gluck stopped laughing and said abruptly, "So *this* is the writer-director you recommend?" With her sitting right there. I mumbled something stupid, and she snapped, "I've already told Mr. Gluck I'm not up for the job—my own company has two movies in development," and Ishmael came in and told Gluck that his Gulfstream had landed and the copilot said they should leave at once, winds were bad. So he soon left with bare good-byes.

Warshaw and Jacobs left in a limo, Solovei drove off with Arnold Granit. Granit is a little guy with a tired face who's made huge films. Speaking of tired, I quit right here and reel off to bed.

MARGOLIT SOLOVEI ENTERPRISES LLC
10235 SUNSET BOULEVARD
LOS ANGELES, CA 90077

Dear Josh:

Well. I owe you an account of what happened last night at the curry party, since you were the first to let me know it was on.

In a word, it was weird. It started off very badly, Warshaw and Jacobs arrived together and sat around making clumsy small talk with me, the Wouks, and Arnold Granit. Arnold's my former producer and my confidant, going on seventy. You've probably seen a couple of his big musicals and historical epics. We flew down but it was windy as hell coming through the pass, a scary landing, and we hired a car at the airport to drive back.

Gluck came in late when we'd started eating. He showed up with his aborigine caregiver pushing him in a wheelchair. As Mrs. Wouk welcomed him and they chatted, he scanned the room and made a beeline for me. Wouk came over, introduced us and ducked, and there I was with an Australian billionaire who put on a yarmulke to eat. Very bright old gent, blue wise eyes, nice crinkly-eyed smile, odd Aussie-Jewish accent. I liked him. We hadn't been talking too long, just this and that, when he up and says, "Aren't you Pearl Nightingale?" I caught my breath, "Why do you ask?"

Turned out he'd seen *Bobover, Bobover* in New York—someone told him it was a funny Jewish play. Said I looked like the playwright's picture on the cover. Well, what could I say? Maybe the old fox figured out it's a translation of my name, or he ran a check on me. God knows what else he found out, but this was enough. I told him yes, I was Pearl Nightingale. His face turned stony. "That was a very, very bad play."

"It was my first effort that got produced."

"Why did you write it?"

"At the time I thought it was funny."

"Why did you use a false name as author?"

"I didn't want my father to hear that I wrote it."

He turns on the scowl of a destroying angel. "So, you had that much respect for your father?"

"I still do."

"But not enough respect to keep you from writing such a play."

"Not at the time."

"And now?"

"I revere my father, always will. We move in different worlds."

Then the most amazing thing happens. This frightening old moneybags bursts out laughing. "Did your father really tear up your library cards? Wake you up every midnight to learn Hasidic philosophy?" Those gimlet eyes were now merry as Santa Claus. "I'm a Gerrer Hasid—we don't think too much of the Bobovers. Your Tatti must have been a trial." At that point Wouk came over, and Gluck turned on the destroying angel look. "So this is the writer-director you recommend?"

As Wouk stammered a comment (he was kind of bleary, past his bedtime maybe), I interjected that I wasn't up for the job and in fact wasn't interested, I'd come to the meeting just to find out why I was invited. I called over Arnold Granit. "Here's your man," I said to Gluck. "Nobody makes better big films, he'll get the best writers—"

I hadn't prepped Arnold, I was just snatching at a straw to cover the awkward moment. Arnold said through his teeth, "Forget it, Margo," and his tone ended it. Gluck's aborigine wheeled him away to murmur with Jacobs and Warshaw in a corner, probably about Wouk's idiocy in considering me. Anyway, the thing broke up in dismal good-byes all around. I've waited a week before writing you about it. Not a word from anyone! In this town such silence tends to be a kaddish over a dead deal.

So what? It was always a brainstorm, I'm probably well out of it. Thanks for tipping me off, without a word about my unsuitability for a Bible epic.

Always affectionately,

Margo

MARGO SNAGS MOSES

October 21. WarshaWorks has signed phenom Margolit Solovei to write and direct a Moses epic, *The Lawgiver*. A Houston venture capitalist and an Australian uranium tycoon are backing the film. Solovei's previous credits are the art-house comedies *Zuleika Dobson* and The *Unbearable Bassington*, and a college-chick-flick, *Barnard Blues*. She wrote her first two films for Universal's Arnold Granit, and then formed *(Turn to page 2)*

GRANIT PRODUCTIONS
10 CENTURY PLAZA
CENTURY CITY, CA 90067

(By hand—Personal & Confidential)

From: Arnold Granit
To: Margolit Solovei

Received your smarmy e-mail, Margo, and let's have no more of this *I regard you as my father* stuff, understand? I've seen *Daily Variety*, and I'm mad as hell. You've behaved like an idiot, plunged into an ill-advised commitment, and now you want my "input"! If you can still wiggle out of this folly, do so. Tim Warshaw is an operator. Because Wouk hasn't said yes or no yet, Tim jumped the gun and tied you up. This project is beyond you, Margo. You've made small films, not bad ones. Maybe in five, ten years you'll have learned enough to take on a Moses movie, if anyone's interested then. Rescue yourself, sink yourself. Not my concern.

Arnie

Shayna Daniels on location in Turkey.
Tim Warshaw in Cedars-Sinai Medical Center, Los Angeles.

WARSHAW: Hi, you called?

DANIELS: Oh, hi! So you're sitting out on the lawn now. That's good. I've been worried about your relapse—

WARSHAW: Yes, it's a warm day. Sun feels good—

DANIELS: Say, Tim, are you out of your bloody skull? Jacobs faxed me the *Daily Variety* front page. *Margo Solovei* for Moses?

WARSHAW: I know what I'm doing, Shayna. That's a pretty scarf—

DANIELS: Don't dodge—Margo's an artsy-craftsy lightweight, you know that, and her college comedy is just warmed-over Wendy Wasserstein. She's all right, but *Moses?!* Come on, Tim!

WARSHAW: I told you about the curry meeting—

DANIELS: Yes, so what?

WARSHAW: Ever since, Hezzie Jacobs has been on my case. Hezzie says he never saw Gluck eat anything outside his home but hard-boiled eggs and salads, but he ate Mrs. Wouk's curry, he must trust her on short acquaintance. Maybe that put him in a good mood, because the vibes I got from that old poker face were pro-Margo. All I've done is tie her up for a while. I had to keep Hezzie happy, you know that. How's the work going?

DANIELS: Okay, in fact excellent. Yesterday we shot Achilles dragging Hector's body around the walls of Troy. That Roman ruin we're using looks terrific in the dailies. Bronko found a perfect Achilles in London, this huge tall galoot from Australia. He's scary—he's so fierce and bloodthirsty in action, and off-camera so meek and quiet. His name's Perry Pines, and my Turkish assistant director keeps getting his name wrong. "Retake three, Mr. Penis." That breaks everybody up, I have to correct him, more giggles. *(They both laugh.)* Perry's a find, pity he's just got this one scene at the beginning—is that your nurse?

WARSHAW: Yes. Look, Shayna, now that I've got Margo, I believe I can get Wouk. If I get Wouk, I get Gluck. That's bingo, and that's the caper. Keep your shirtwaist on. Talk to you later.

Whew, did BSW give me a hard time over dinner tonight about that *Daily Variety* story! She says my foot is caught in a trap I set myself, that note to Warshaw I dashed off and Gluck pounced on. All I wrote was that I'd *consider* a writer-director. I did put it on paper and I did sign my name, signed two more copies at Gluck's request, and that was that, she says. Gluck can read people. He knew he had me then and there.

Well, maybe. I've held off turning down Solovei because I sense in her a shadow of aptness for the job. BSW challenged me abrasively on that. Perhaps I just find the woman fetching? "For crying out loud," I protested, "at my age?" She raked me with a claw, "No fool like an old fool." That's BSW. In fact, I *am* taken with Margo. Her looks are nice, but mainly the knowing amused irony in her eyes, the quick graceful hand gestures, sort of bring back the BSW I encountered sixty-odd years ago in San Pedro during a navy yard overhaul. Smart deep women are rare. Anyway, I said I'd stalled because I knew Margo couldn't handle an epic film, it needed an old hand, a William Wyler, a Victor Fleming, nowadays an Arnold Granit. "Well, then, *call* Granit," says she. "He knows Solovei. At the curry meeting I talked a lot with him. He thinks the idea of her doing Moses is ridiculous. Ask him point-blank! If he tells you so himself, that's that, you can tell Warshaw you're out."

I'll call Granit tomorrow.

Chapter Three
MARGO'S MOSES

Wouk called me about the *Daily Variety* story.

Can we talk right away?

Arnie

WARSHAW: Look, Arnie, why not give it a thought, since it's Wouk's idea?

GRANIT: Surely you're not serious! I've had three writers working on *Remembrance Rock* for months. Also, I have a green light from Universal to develop *Quo Vadis*, and—

WARSHAW: Okay, okay, Arnold. If you can lick that huge Carl Sandburg cinder block, my hat's off to you. *Quo Vadis*, well, Mervyn LeRoy's picture's a classic, a remake is a remake . . . are you listening to the buzz about Moses?

GRANIT: Nine days' wonder. It'll die down.

WARSHAW: Think so? I don't. If you're so sure it's beyond Margo, why not go ahead and tell Wouk yourself?

GRANIT: What for? To take the rap for crushing her hopes? Not me.

WARSHAW: Well, it's Wouk putting you in that bind, not me! I'm quite serious, you and Margo together could make one hell of a Moses film—Oh, sorry—that's her on the other line now. . . .

MARGOLIT SOLOVEI ENTERPRISES LLC
10235 SUNSET BOULEVARD
LOS ANGELES, CA 90077

Dear Mr. Wouk:

Your invitation was a welcome surprise. Please thank Mrs. Wouk again for the delicious lunch, much more than I usually eat at midday. The quiche was irresistible.

Herewith a few notes on *The Lawgiver*. You were right, I had to put my notions on paper, and in fact they took form as I went. Just thinking about actually doing the film almost paralyzes me, but I know what I want to accomplish. I hope these notes convey the beginnings of a vision.

If you remain interested, please remember that Mr. Gluck's idea of your controlling my work is not acceptable.

Sincerely,

Margolit Solovei

Notes Toward a Screen Treatment on *The Lawgiver*

(Confidential—for Herman Wouk's eyes only!)

When we first met I told you that the Moses story was "two *Lawrence of Arabias* in length." Well, I was talking through my hat. I hadn't opened a Bible since I left home at seventeen, and when I reread the Torah for my job interview with you, I was bowled over by the sheer storytelling power. That's not how the Torah was taught to me, not in childhood, not till the day I broke away for good. "We believe it," my father said about Moses' staff that turns into a snake. "I can't believe it," I said. "You *must* believe it," said Tatti ("Daddy" in Yiddish). That afternoon I packed up, went to New York, and got a job and a room.

Now that I face filming this marvelous story, instinct says, "Three and a half hours, maximum." Genesis is a prologue, Deuteronomy is a review. The Moses action that matters all transpires in three books, not five—Exodus, Leviticus, and Numbers —and of those three, less than half is storytelling, the rest is religious law. *Gone With the Wind* length, no more: bursts of hard action, *huge* time lapses—that's how the Torah tells it. That's how the film will tell it, from the beguiling entrance of Moses as a crying baby in a basket to the pathos of the hoary Lawgiver's exit, alone on Mount Nebo, glimpsing the Promised Land with dying eyes.

Cecil B. DeMille was a potentate of old Hollywood, where Captain Ahab killed Moby Dick and peg-legged it gaily home to his sweetheart, and Anna Karenina and Vronsky lived happily ever after. In DeMille's *Ten Commandments*, the Bible narrative is good for about forty minutes, mainly mob scenes and special effects— pretty good for 1956. The story is a love triangle: Moses, Pharaoh, and an Egyptian tootsie, Nefretiri, who is no more in the Torah than Aphrodite or my Aunt Sadie. Sheer horsefeathers. No character or story element will be in our film that's not in the Bible.

One major point: without the prologue in Genesis, the story of Moses hangs in the air, meaningless. Who are these "children of Israel" that he frees? How do they come to be in Egypt? Why are they slaves? I think of a majestic voice-over doing a PowerPoint talk with Gustave Doré's Genesis engravings to Bach organ music: creation of light, Adam and Eve, Noah's ark, Abraham seeing Sodom destroyed, sacrifice of Isaac, Joseph advising Pharaoh, Jacob's family arriving in Egypt, and so on. Purpose of this ten-minute prelude, to wake in audiences—Christian, Jewish, and Muslim alike—childhood memories of religious teachings.

Hmmm —
Not bad, lively
intelligence at
work—

Rock I to Rock II: The Structure

My father often said, "Seventy faces to the Torah." I perceive a "face" of Moses far from the traditions pumped into me from childhood on, and just as far from DeMille's presumptuous foolery. If you don't buy this face, I don't get the job, and will probably be relieved, once I've cried my eyes out. Meantime, here it is.

There are two scenes in the Moses story, one near the beginning, one near the end, that seem the same. On the march to Sinai through the desert, the newly freed slaves demand water, Moses strikes a rock with his staff, and ample water flows forth. Forty years later a new generation, about to fight its way into the Promised Land, makes trouble over a water shortage, and again Moses strikes a rock and produces water. The Bible critics I devoured as a teenager, in the public library's *Encyclopaedia Britannica*, probably say that it's the same scene narrated in two different "documents." As I recall, there are no such documents, it's all conjecture and surmise, but anyway, that's dead wrong. The two episodes are actually very different, and the difference defines Moses the Lawgiver.

The Young Moses

Through a montage of "history moments" —Pharaoh ordering the enslavement, mothers screaming as babies are torn away and thrown into the Nile, slaves at hard labor—Moses' mother and sister float the basket among the Nile reeds, Pharaoh's daughter retrieves and opens the basket, bonds to the baby at sight, says with love and tenderness, "A Hebrew boy," and gives the baby to his mother to wet-nurse. The princess's Hebrew foster son briefly skylarks around the palace, then metamorphoses into young Moses, tall, magnificent, in his first venture beyond the royal compound to see "his brothers." He has never forgotten who he is, absorbed with his mother's milk. He sees a task-master clubbing a slave, "looks here and there" (perfect Torah touch!), kills him, and buries him in the sand. Next day he comes on two Jews fighting. When he tries to intervene, the bad one sneers, "Oh, kill me, will you, as you killed the Egyptian?" So the word is out, he must flee Pharaoh's wrath. In distant Midian he encounters the daughters of the High Priest, marries one, and becomes a herdsman, tending the flocks of his father-in-law.

The Epic Begins!

In a breathtaking storytelling leap, the next Torah verses depict Moses as Michelangelo and Rembrandt saw him, a mighty bearded stalwart of eighty! He is grazing his flock in a mountain wilderness, sees a bush on fire—strange enough in this uninhabited pasture—and observes that the fire keeps flaming and flaming, doesn't burn out, and approaches for a closer look. "Moses, Moses!" a disembodied voice calls.

Is he startled? *Not in the least.* He recognizes that Voice! For forty years, alone under the sun and stars, he has been meditating on the God of Abraham, Isaac, Jacob, Joseph, the whole sacred family history taught him by his mother, before she had to relinquish him to the princess. "Here I am," he says to thin air, and the epic begins.

How? With his pleading unfitness for the task God wants him to do—deliver the slaves out of Egypt and lead them to the Promised Land. Five times he tries to beg off, hardly a hero in the ancient mold of Homer or Plutarch. In a later scene the Torah will say of him, *"The man Moses was humbler than all men on earth."* Moses the self-doubting Deliverer, believing in God but never in himself, from this first moment to the climax and final disaster at Rock II—that's the face of the Lawgiver I see and was never taught.

OK— Read the rest later. Get in touch with Gluck!

Hezzie,

It's imperative I contact Louis Gluck at once and direct, NOT through any Hollywood contacts. Ask him to get in touch with me, highest urgency.

From: Herman Wouk
To: Louis Gluck

Thanks for your swift response to Hezzie's message. I've never been to Brazil. Sorry I've missed Rio, now I'm not up to such long air travel. I don't know how you do it, even in your Gulfstream.

Herewith I've attached Margolit Solovei's notes on her proposed Lawgiver movie. Your intent to honor Moses in an epic film is fine, but on the basis of these notes, I'm sorry to say that I can't recommend your taking on such a colossal expense, not unless you yourself see merit enough in Solovei's unorthodox "face" of Moses to proceed. Solovei is not a major filmmaker by any means, you know that, and surely you've sized up Warshaw as a spender and a plunger. Your call.

Mr. Wouk, I can't make anything of those notes. If you're in, I'm in. If you're out, I'm out. Ask your wife.

GRANIT: I can't say I understand you. To begin with, you tell me she marked those notes "Confidential—for Herman Wouk's eyes only!" You're violating a confidence.

WOUK: For sufficient reason.

GRANIT: Which is what?

WOUK: It's the only way forward. Otherwise, I drop out, so Gluck drops out. Margo loses her big chance and is left with a misleading head-line in *Daily Variety* and a lot of egg on her face—

GRANIT: Well deserved.

WOUK: Maybe not. Read her notes and then tell me that.

GRANIT: Why should I?

WOUK: Why should I be in this at all, Mr. Granit?

GRANIT: That's Arnold. . . . Look, Mr. Wouk, with all respect, I'm furious at Margolit Solovei, she's been a damned idiot, and I'm extremely busy. I'll have to get back to you. Good-bye.

**MARGOLIT SOLOVEI ENTERPRISES LLC
10235 SUNSET BOULEVARD
LOS ANGELES, CA 90077**

Dearest Josh,

This is shockingly out of line, but will you come out here and talk to me? How long has it been, four, five years? Or seven? I'm in over my head, I'm in acute panic, I trust nobody here, I may lose the big breakthrough of my life, and it's too complicated for phone talk or e-mails. Your first-class flight, your hotel, and everything will be on me and don't you get huffy, also whatever your hourly rate, that's on me, too, because this is a cri de coeur for legal counsel. The Margo you knew, Josh dear, the stiff-necked self-reliant toughie, is at the moment just a damsel in distress.

Always,

Mashie

Lewin, Rubinstein & Curtis
1440 K Street, NW
Washington, DC 20005

Joshua Lewin, Senior Partner

Mashie—

I'm writing on the red-eye back to Washington. In my fleeting stop at your office on the way to LAX, there was no time to tell you any of this. Since you put my visit (and are paying for it) on a business basis, this is a business letter. Just a personal word first. Damsel in distress, my eye. Jane Austen in Hollywood! Crushing you in my arms wouldn't have been to the purpose, but the fact is I find you in the flesh more bewitching than ever, with the poise that comes with years of success. As to our old standoff, your rueful, hurried good-bye kiss was sweet beyond words, and painful. Too poignant a flash of former days. It'll last me for a while.

I met Warshaw and the Texas moneyman, Hezzie Jacobs, at the WarshaWorks offices in Century City. Warshaw strikes me as a quick-witted manipulator, straightway invited me into their conversation and said sugary things about you. This Hezzie looks like my Uncle Mendel and drawls like John Wayne. Sheldon Rubinstein is handling minor patent issues for his Nullarbor project, something about algae, and from the little Sheldon told me, it sounds as nutty as the movie business. A piece of work, Hezzie Jacobs.

My meeting with Granit was the real eye-opener. Once he talked, he really talked! In sum, Granit has taken your ditching him (as he put it) and forming your own company very hard. When I suggested that he'd become a sort of father figure and you wanted to grow up, he exploded. "Not at all, nonsense! Pure selfishness and ingratitude!" The overwrought tone was the giveaway. Rich and prominent sure, but Arnold Granit is not a happy man. Your real reason for quitting him became self-evident. He's in love with you. That would be his problem, except that now you need him, and that's your problem. That's why you sent for me. And that I responded—and always will—is my problem.

In the Wikipedia entry on Granit, he comes out as a notable figure of the bygone time of DeMille and Busby Berkeley. If he's read it, it's bound to irk him. I made two points, and though he couldn't have been more cold and bristly, he listened. I pointed out, first, that only someone with his experience and power could make an up-to-date Bible epic, and second, that nowadays, a Moses film costing hundreds of millions could be fully funded up front only by a freak chance like this Australian Hasid's whim . . .

Mashie, the flight attendant just jogged me, landing at Dulles Airport in 30 minutes. Two red-eyes in a row have been a bit much, I've slept three uneasy hours, laptop open on my lap. To wrap this up fast, Granit was grudging and unfriendly to the last, but he will get in touch with Wouk and will read your "confidential" notes. I hope I've helped, since that's what you said you wanted. You can't make a Moses film without Granit, you've realized that yourself. As for fending off a man in love with you, I'd say, in your showbiz jargon, that you've got the chops.

My hourly rate is $800, bill will be along.

Always yours,

Josh

From: Margolit Solovei
To: Joshua Lewin
Subject: Hosannah!

Glory be, Josh, you can do anything, can't you? Arnie tells me he's going to see Wouk! It doesn't mean I'm home yet, but what a relief! I have no words for my gratitude. Full disclosure, I can tell you that the kiss worked for me, too, worked like all hell, but don't go building on that. Nothing really changed, you kissed a preoccupied pagan.

Love,

Mashie

From: Joshua Lewin
To: Margolit Solovei

Mashie,

Glad I moved Granit a bit.

I write this during a ten-minute recess in court. Shelly Rubinstein is down with flu, and I'm here to get a continuance on a lawsuit against Uncle Mendel, a.k.a. Hezzie Jacobs. The Weizmann Institute in Israel has entered the case, quite a development. Seems Hezzie pilfered (or didn't pilfer) the "genetically engineered algae molecule" of an Institute geneticist, Dr. Marvin Zivoni. Anything with a Zionist aroma draws New York reporters like wasps. One even pounced on me, null result. I just hope they don't get to Hezzie in Houston. God knows what algae doubletalk he might drawl.

Preoccupied pagan, I love you.

Josh

Moses Film Memo #3: Granit's Visit

The fat's in the fire. Granit showed up here and declined coffee or a drink. "No thanks, just let me see those notes." I'd offered to fax them to him, but no. He took my usual armchair and read the pages slowly, one by one, in dour silence. Not much fazes BSW, she went on reading an article in *Vanity Fair* that his arrival had interrupted. I was on edge, torn between hoping for a turn-down that would free me from this nuisance once and for all, and foolishly rooting for Solovei. He put aside the pages and sat there saying nothing, staring off into space for a minute or two. "I understand you're working on a Moses novel," he said at last.

"Thinking about it is nearer right. I've been thinking about it for decades."

"Would it be anything resembling that stuff?"

"Hardly. But 'seventy faces to the Torah,' as she says."

"Yes, quoting the father she abandoned." He turns to BSW. "Mrs. Wouk, I suppose you've read these notes."

She puts her magazine down. "Yes, I have."

"Well, what do you think?"

77

Pause. Delphic opacity, the woman's specialty. "Very strange."

He persists. "I miss my wife. I miss her a lot. Suppose you were my wife. What would you say about my taking on this project?"

"I'd say you want to be persuaded."

He blinks. "Is *that* what you think? I'll take that drink now, thanks. Scotch on the rocks."

That was pretty much it. He unbent over drinks, said nothing remotely resembling a decision, mainly reservations about Margo and the notes. "They're nothing," he said. "Strange, all right, and she has to write a whole shooting script in that vein. DeMille had four writers working on different segments of *The Ten Commandments* for a year and a half. She has no conception of the scope and magnitude of this project. It's a Normandy landing. As for the budget, the Houston man isn't in that class. The Australian Hasid is for real, all right, but he has yet to put up one dollar in cash. I hope you realize that. A fellow that old can pop off overnight." He caught BSW's amused glance at me. "Present company excepted, clearly." With that, he left.

"Will he do it?" I asked BSW.

"I hope not," she said. "He'd be crazy."

Chapter Four

ALGAE AND ACHILLES

(E-MAIL)

From: Hezzie Jacobs
To: Louis Gluck
Subject: Algae molecule

Louie, for God's sake cool down. So the wire services picked up that stupid *New York Post* story, so what? The reporter pestered me on the phone for half an hour and twisted everything I said, so what? It's all good publicity for Nullarbor Petroleum. I could never do anything to damage Israeli interests, you know that. We have a great international law firm on the case, Lewin, Rubinstein and Curtis. Put this thing from your mind. Bill Gillespie, my genetics consultant, is a full professor emeritus of Cornell. He called me from Nullarbor Ponds, where he is now chief of production. "Post-Doc grad of mine, Marvin Zivoni," Bill said. "Good man, but wrong on the molecules."

Look, Louie, Tim Warshaw has been phoning me again. Preproduction costs are now well over budget, and he will need another substantial advance. I appreciate your partial refunding of my early advances to WarshaWorks, but please pay me the balance now in view of this Zivoni thing. I'm stretched very thin, and such nonsense at worst can lead to high legal costs.

All best,

Hezzie

From: Louis Gluck
To: Hezzie Jacobs

I know the Lewin law firm, it's tops. Just make sure Lewin himself handles this business, he did a brilliant job for me on Ukraine Titanium. About Warshaw's preproduction overrun, send me the numbers.

Gluck

The Ahwahnee Hotel
1 Ahwahnee Road
Yosemite National Park, CA 95389

Margo here, I'm holed up to preserve my sanity. Now and then in recent weeks I've almost regretted that Arnold took on the production. He's been working me like a horse, and he's turned slave driver. Pages, *pages!* Now, *now!* Then he berates me because they're so rough. He wasn't like this at all on *Zuleika* or *Bassington*, now he says those were five-finger exercises, *this* is making moving pictures.

Your wife as agent has a heart of stone, and that man Gluck drives a devil's bargain. I'm agonizingly aware that I have to finish the screenplay and only *then* show it to you, and only *then* will Mr. Gluck fund the production, providing you approve. So far I like my screenplay. Last night at 2 a.m. I finished the Golden Calf sequence. Now I dread showing the pages to Arnold. I tried to avoid DeMille's striptease orgy and retain the splendor of the spectacle, climaxing in the great shot of Moses smashing the Tablets— out of *grief,* not rage, *grief* and despair at his failure as a leader. That's Rembrandt's insight, not mine, and it's genius, but have I captured it?

I have to ask of you a huge favor, a secret favor. Will you read my screen-play so far as it goes and tell me what you truly think, especially about the Calf scene? This morning when I read the sequence I hated it. I'll be on live coals till I hear from you.

In extremis,

Margo Solovei

Moses Film

Always something! Solovei's letter from Yosemite has muddied my first really exciting new start on the Moses novel in years. Telling the Moses story *from Aaron's viewpoint in diary form* seems a true fresh inspiration. But now here's the bloody *Lawgiver* thing again! How did I ever get into this quagmire? Rabbi Heber got me to see Jacobs, Jacobs got me to see Gluck, and with my own idiot hands I breached my privacy firewall by giving Gluck that fatal note. BSW read the Margo letter with her usual slow care and handed it back. "Nix," she said, a *nix* with icicles on it. We had a short back-and-forth, and she snapped, "At least, tell Granit about it." I did, and taped our talk. (Infected by Hollywood ways, dealing with Hollywood trolls.)

GRANIT: Well, this is out of left field. Did you consult your wife? She dictated the contract that protects you to go on writing your novel. Margo's playing cute.

WOUK: BSW agrees with you. "Pure manipulation," she says. We had words. Upshot, I'm calling you.

GRANIT: Then I say listen to her. Let Margo sweat. I'd welcome your input, sure, but in your place I'd have your wife send her a one-line turndown, referring her to your contract.

When I played back the taped conversation for BSW, she said nothing. At dinner, nothing. No comment till bedtime. After lights-out, no relaxed pillow talk. I had a bad night, and in the morning over coffee in the garden I said, "Okay, I'm letting her send me the stuff—"

"Oh, big surprise! You always do as you please."

"*Listen* to me! I'll comment only on the Golden Calf scene. That's all she asked for. You'll vet my response before I send it. How's that?"

"Come, Candy, it's getting windy out here." And into the house she stalked with her dopey golden retriever.

Moses Film

Sunday.

Well, the screenplay so far isn't hopeless. The ten-minute "PowerPoint" prologue through the Book of Genesis using the Gustave Doré engravings could work. For the Burning Bush and the revelation on Sinai, God talks *Hebrew,* with English subtitles. Simple, smart. In *The Ten Commandments*, God spoke a pompous pulpit English. Granit is scouring opera companies, she notes, for a basso profundo to do God. Her best stroke is picking up on the prophetess Miriam as she leads out the women with timbrels in a victory dance, on the Red Sea shore lined with broken chariots and drowned Egyptians and horses. Hard upon this, with Moses off on the mountain, comes the Golden Calf revelry—same dancers, skimpy costumes, orgiastic music, cavorting half-naked men added. This powerful transit is right there in the Torah. DeMille missed it entirely. She's run with it.

I'm mentioning the few good things. It's all a colossal gamble, Louis Gluck's gamble, not mine, and at some point he must face it. Will today's audiences stay with such a movie? The Torah narrative is not popcorn amusement for dating teenagers, that's for sure, yet no other story compares to it. The New Testament rests on it, the Koran recapitulates it, the whole world reads it. By comparison, who reads the Mahabharata, or the Bhagavad Gita, or for that matter the *Iliad*? Granting a billionaire's obsession that a Moses movie must get made, Solovei's pass at it may do as well as any, but Moses so dominates it that casting the part is a mile-high hurdle. The actor in this movie would have to *disappear* into the part. My old departed friend Charlton Heston, whether as Ben-Hur, Michelangelo, or Moses, was always one and the same statuesque Chuck Heston.

BSW took half a day to read the pages. Handing them back to me, she made a face. "Shallow. Shallow."

"What attempt at Moses wouldn't be shallow?"

"Yours, if you'd ever write it."

MARGO

Yosemite, Thursday

Mr. Wouk,

Your prompt return of my script is appreciated. I hoped for a broader comment, but it's nice to know that, as per your brief covering note, the Golden Calf scene "can work." Under your wife's stringent script contract, you didn't have to respond at all, so I thank you.

Sincerely,

M. Solovei

SHIRLEY JUNG SCHARF

Dear Margo Solovei:

A voice from the long, long ago! I've just read in the Hadassah Newsletter about your Moses film, and I'm sooo excited! Cast your mind back to Bais Yaakov high school, Mashie, where you and I were best friends. Yes, I'm the same Shirley, only now a mama of three, so a bit plumpish. In the Hadassah photo you look so pretty and slim! I've seen all your movies, and kept clippings about you. My hubby, Arthur (Avram) Scharf, was in Joshua Lewin's class at Yeshiva High. Josh of course is quite the big Washington lawyer now. Arthur's in my father's real estate firm and very happy.

I'm writing, actually, because last night we ran into Joshua at the new Broadway hit, the Russell Crowe <u>Hamlet</u>. The lobby was jammed, and who comes pushing through the crowd but Josh, calling "Avram, Avram!" They hugged, and it was as though no time had passed. Josh introduced us to this girl, Deborah. It takes one Bais Yaakov girl to spot another, and she was one, no doubt of it, lovely red hair in a ponytail, understated makeup, long skirt but not too long, "kosher," you know. She's no knockout, but I'd say quietly sexy, that type. She teaches English Lit at NYU. So many years since you and I both had a crush on Josh Lewin. Now he's losing his hair. Do you ever hear from him?

Someday when you're in New York, maybe we can have lunch and talk over old times. I'd love that.

As ever,

Shirley

Bernard Solovei, Importer
1230 Main Street
Passaic, New Jersey 07055

Mr. Joshua Lewin
Lewin, Rubinstein & Curtis
1440 K Street, NW
Washington, DC 20009

Dear Josh:

You remember me, I'm sure—Margolit's brother. Our father is terribly upset by a report in a Brooklyn Yiddish biweekly that a daughter of the Passaic Bobover Rebbe is making a film about Moses. Tatti has never in his life seen a film and never will. All he knows by Yiddish hearsay is that all movies are full of dirty words and men and women doing it naked. If you can fill me in with anything I can tell Tatti, I'd be thankful. At least Mashie knows the Torah. When I was a yeshiva boy I saw a Bible movie on the sneak, *Samson and Delilah.* When I told the guys at the yeshiva about it, they pretty near died laughing.

It was a sad day when you two broke up. Tatti never approved, but the rest of us secretly did, even my mother. In fact she's still hoping, since she's heard you remain single.

Sincerely,

Bernard "Beshie" Solovei

From: Joshua Lewin
To: Margolit Solovei

Dear Mashie:

Attached, a letter I got from your brother Beshie. Maybe you should write to him yourself. I frankly don't know much more about *The Lawgiver* than the trade papers report.

Incidentally, thanks for paying my bill. My lawyer's heart rejoices, of course, at any fee from any hand, but I felt stupid depositing your check. Henceforth let's drop this lawyer-client charade. You know perfectly well I'm yours to command whenever I can be helpful.

As ever,

Josh

From: Margolit Solovei
To: Joshua Lewin

Yosemite, Tuesday

Josh dear,

I'm up to my ears in urgent script work. Please answer Beshie yourself, just use your discretion.

Now, how about this Deborah who teaches at NYU? Shirley Scharf wrote me about your encounter at the theater. First time I've heard from Shirley since Bais Yaakov days. Shirley described her, red hair in a ponytail and all, and made her sound damned attractive. Dear old Shirley.

You're sweet to offer free legal service, but I'll pay you when I should. You earned that fee with your red-eye round-trip. Arnold Granit is now lashing me along like Ben-Hur in the chariot race.

Ever,

Mashie

From: Josh
To: Mashie

Debbie is indeed attractive. Her fiancé, Cy Diamond, is serving in Afghanistan. When Cy and I were counselors in a boys' camp, we'd take flying lessons once a week at a nearby small airport. I never soloed, but Cy did, and kept it up even while he was earning his MBA at Yale. Sort of a flying nut, he joined the Air Force Reserve and so he got called up for Afghanistan, where he's a helicopter pilot. I like Debbie, a bookish sort. Shirley has sure put on the pounds.

More power to Granit. You can use a little lashing.

Arts

Moses Breaking the Tablets of the Law
Gustave Doré

MOVIES

SCARLETT O'MOSES?

The ambitious, hugely costly epic *The Lawgiver*, already piling up massive preproduction costs at WarshaWorks, has an intractable casting problem in Moses, Man of the Lord. Who can play this giant figure? Clint Eastwood is reportedly interested in playing Pharaoh, which if true raises the bar even higher. One version of the buzz: Warshaw met Eastwood at the Broadway opening of the Russell Crowe *Hamlet*, and Eastwood was overheard opining that Pharaoh was the great part, the hard-nosed human being who takes on God. Unconfirmed reports leak about hush-hush approaches to superstars, but the power agents are not talking. Meantime veteran epic producer Arnold Granit *(Xenophon, Fall of Jerusalem)* has a casting call out to theater companies coast to coast. Scouts send likely prospects on to Granit, who meets them one-on-one and gives screen tests to a very few. Margolit Solovei *(Barnard Blues, Zuleika Dobson)* is drafting the screenplay, an unlikely choice for writer-director, dictated by murky WarshaWorks financing. Australian uranium mogul Louis Gluck (see p. 17)

DANIELS: Hi, Tim, just got your urgent e-mail, what's up? It's past midnight here. Great *Time* story—

WARSHAW: Maybe, but this Moses thing is killing me, I should never have gotten into it—

DANIELS: You do look lousy, are you sure you're over that duodenal ulcer?

WARSHAW: Who knows? I feel terrible, I need another physical. Total stymie on Moses. Tom Hanks is out, mulling a high post in the Department of Defense. Crowe is out, he intends to tour his sensational *Hamlet*—look, Shayna, that actor you used for Achilles, where is he now?

DANIELS: Pines? He went back to London ages ago.

WARSHAW: Call his agent and get hold of him.

DANIELS: Really? All right, first thing in the morning—

WARSHAW: *Now!* I've been racking and racking my brains. At three a.m. I snapped awake remembering what you said about this big galoot, so meek and quiet off-camera and so powerful as Achilles—

DANIELS: Tim, cool it, you sound frantic—

WARSHAW: Don't aggravate me, call the agent now!

DANIELS: Okay, okay!

(Later that day.)

WARSHAW: Now what? I'm out the door to the hospital.

DANIELS: Perry Pines is in Australia.

WARSHAW: Jesus.

DANIELS: His agent was pretty shitty at being waked up, Tim. He said, and I quote, "The overgrown sod is back on his father's sheep farm, where he belongs." Look, Tim, Perry is just a bit player—

WARSHAW: For Christ's sake, Shayna, contact the guy somehow. And *now!* Do you hear?

DANIELS: *(laughs)* I hear and I obey, master.

Crooked Creek Farm
RMB 6432, Timboon
Victoria, Australia 3268

Dear Ms. Daniels,

Thanks! Frankly, when I received your e-mail I thought I was dreaming! I'd read the *Time* story about *The Lawgiver* and had a brief wistful moment about going for the gold. But the fact is I am all through with acting. In the Little Theatre movement in Australia, I did pretty well for years. I received my best notices for my Othello, and my Henry Higgins was once compared to Rex Harrison's. My father was reconciled to my acting and supported me. I brought a large scrapbook of my reviews to London, and went looking for an agent. It was an unlucky day when I signed with Geoffrey Smallweed. He pigeonholed me from the start as a "hunk," nothing but six feet four of beefcake. But he was all smooth London show business talk, and I went and signed a five-year contract that tied me up hand and foot, fool that I was. He kept getting me muscleman parts in low-budget vulgar films, which I did because I had to eat. On an impulse I went on my own to your London tryouts and lucked into the part of Achilles, it was my one taste of real acting in three years, and you can bet Geoff Smallweed collected his 20 percent all the same! That was it. I turned down some more of those hunk parts, then I flew home when my dad took sick. I've rediscovered the farm life of my youth, and the sheep I've always loved, and my native sweet, fresh air after two years of the smelly, gloomy London murk. I couldn't be more contented, I'm where I belong and my stagestruck days are over.

I do appreciate the nice things Mr. Warshaw told you about my Achilles. (He had to look fast to see me!) I hope *Aeneas and Dido* will be a blockbuster, and thanks again, but I am not interested.

Sincerely,

Perry Michael Pines

From: Tim Warshaw
To: Perry Pines

Dear Perry Pines:

Will pay you $20,000 + all expenses for 2 weeks' screen testing. No fee to Geoffrey Smallweed, my London attorney guarantees.

Timothy Warshaw

From: Perry Pines
To: Tim Warshaw

Dear Mr. Warshaw:

I will arrive LAX Thursday, Qantas Flight 23A.

Perry Michael Pines

Chapter Five

PLAN B

From: Mashie
To: Josh

Hi—

Thanks for writing to Beshie. You did reassure him about my films, and he sort of reassured Tatti by quoting you. Tatti never approved of you, but he respected your brains.

On this morning's news I saw where a helicopter has disappeared over Afghanistan. Cy Diamond's fiancée must be distraught, but in fact such aviators can turn up alive. A nephew of my cinematographer on *Bassington* went missing in a fighter plane, and later search planes found him alive in the mountains. Maybe mention this story to your friend, it might comfort her. If I knew her, I'd write to her myself.

I'm about halfway through my screenplay, exhilarated and despairing by turns as I go.

All best,

Mashie

JOSHUA LEWIN

Mashie,

Bad news, it <u>was</u> Cy's helo. The Air Force notified Debbie before the media got the story. She'd be much comforted, I think, if you did write her. She's a real fan of yours. Her address is

Deborah Kamaiko
97 West 104th Street
New York, NY 10025

"Distraught" isn't a word I'd apply to Debbie, she keeps her feelings to herself, but of course the news about Cy is a body blow.

Carry on with that screenplay and get it done. You're in it now. Any progress on "Scarlett O'Moses"? He's certainly getting good coverage in the media.

Josh

Chateau Marmont

8221 Sunset Boulevard
Hollywood, California 90046

Dear Dad,

Well, here I am in Hollywood, in this famous hotel where so many stars have stayed that I hesitate to use the hotel's stationery, I feel like an imposter! When I arrived, Mr. Warshaw himself met me in a limousine with the writer-director, Ms. Solovei, and they booked me into this big suite. However, since then I'm just sitting here, no word from Mr. Warshaw or anyone else. Day before yesterday I called his office, asking what I should do next. His secretary said he was on a conference call and would call me back. He hasn't yet. In the limo Ms. Solovei, the writer-director, was very nice to me, she asked about sheep farming and seemed real interested. If I don't hear from Warshaw today I'll try to contact her. I came here mostly because the $20,000 solved our mortgage mess, and what was there to lose?

On the plane I did some daydreaming about how to play Moses, and I was glad you made us read the Bible aloud as kids. What a part! But as the days pass I'm sobering up, I miss the farm, my acting ambitions are dead, and anyway Moses is far beyond the likes of me. If I hadn't taken their money I'd just walk out and come on home, but as it is I'm stuck for ten more days, then home!

Your loving son,

Perry

From: James C. Bearing, barrister
To: Tim Warshaw

Mr. Geoffrey Smallweed has accepted my offer. As an agent he's just a bottom-feeder, his office is in his hat. Pines was an incredible innocent to sign with him. We close this afternoon. I may Skype you later today.

MARGOLIT SOLOVEI ENTERPRISES LLC
10235 SUNSET BOULEVARD
LOS ANGELES, CA 90077

Dear Deborah Kamaiko,

Joshua Lewin gave me your address. I hope this isn't an intrusion. Mike Burris, the cinematographer on my film *The Unbearable Bassington*, had a fighter pilot nephew, Jerry, who disappeared over Iraq. The family was devastated, then search planes found him in the mountains in bad shape but surviving. Burris is an Air Force veteran and he maintained all along that Jerry's chances were good. Last I heard, Jerry was back in the States, recuperating. I hope your fiancé will have the same luck, and I just wanted to share that story with you. I told it to Joshua, and he suggested I write you myself.

Joshua is a very old friend. In the absence of Cy I'm sure you find him cheering company. Where did you go to Bais Yaakov?

Sincerely,

Margolit Solovei

NEW YORK UNIVERSITY

Dear Margolit Solovei:

Thank you for an unexpected and heart-warming letter. Cy has been gone less than two weeks and I'm living on hope. Your story about Jerry Burris couldn't be more welcome.

Now let me confess that I'm excited and charmed to hear from you. I have DVDs of all your films. One by one as they came out they struck me as the work of an enigmatic artist, accessible yet peculiar. You bridge from today's "wise guy" college girls, with perfect pitch for their patois and preoccupations, to neglected English literature that you bring to hot life. How well you caught old Oxford in *Zuleika*, and brought off that preposterously *funny* mass suicide! And how attractive you made that tragic boy-man, Comus Bassington! Even Saki might have approved, austere stylist though he was.

If this is all a gush, so be it. I teach English literature, wrote my thesis on Wilde, of whom, in

110

my view, Beerbohm and Saki are offshoots, or should I say disciples. It has lightened my heart to hear from you, and to write to you. My Bais Yaakov was in the Bronx. I'm a born and bred Bronx girl. My subway stop was Simpson Street, and if you know the Bronx, that should clue you in about my Bais Yaakov school and me.

Again, thanks for your letter.

Sincerely,

Deborah Kamaiko

From: James C. Bearing
To: Tim Warshaw
Subject: Smallweed

A hurried note. Sorry I couldn't raise you on Skype. I'm still sure Smallweed will be no problem. He was delayed yesterday. I hope to close the file on him tomorrow. One serious caution, you were ill-advised to bring Pines to Hollywood just at this stage of the business. My office has watched the internet for a Pines item and so far fortunately has found nothing.

Jim

From: Hezzie Jacobs
To: Louie Gluck

Louie, Bill Gillespie phoned me from Nullarbor, all shook up by legal papers Joshua Lewin sent him to sign. I have every confidence in Lewin on your say-so, but I face unpredictable costs if we actually go to court. So please do think again about refunding at least part of my advances to Warshaw.

(TEXT MESSAGE, DICTATED TO SMODAR BY GLUCK FROM CAPETOWN)

Hezzie—I talked to Lewin. Tell Gillespie to sign the papers. Lewin can handle Zivoni and the Weizmann Institute. The WarshaWorks venture begins to look like a rat hole. Have you been watching the weekly cost reports? I have. Such shleppers! I will visit them soon.
Gluck

Chateau Marmont

8221 Sunset Boulevard
Hollywood, California 90046

Dear Ms. Solovei:

You were very gracious to me in the limo ride from the airport to this celebrated hotel, asking about life on our sheep farm. Mr. Warshaw did most of the talking, of course, and I was almost too awed by him to open my mouth.

I'm puzzled and depressed about what's been going on ever since. You see, I've heard absolutely nothing from Mr. Warshaw or anybody else since I checked in four days ago. The way he talked in the limo, I thought that by now I'd have rehearsed a screen test and maybe actually done it. Has he changed his mind about me because I was so inarticulate, in fact stupid, in the car? Sitting in this posh hotel room all alone, or jogging around Beverly Hills, that thought gnaws at me. Why else don't I hear from him, or from someone?

I'm sending you this fax as a shot in the dark. I'll be thankful to hear from you, believe me. I admired your *Zuleika Dobson* movie a lot. I'd never heard of the book, so I hunted it up. It's a lot of far-fetched fancy-dan writing, but you sure caught the atmosphere of Oxford. When nothing was doing in London for me, I used to take the train to Oxford and just walk around those picturesque old quadrangles, envying the undergrads. Same sort of loneliness I'm feeling here.

Sincerely,

Perry Pines

MARGO

Arnold—

I just had a drink with this Australian actor, Perry Pines, in the Chateau Marmont bar. He's heard from nobody here since Tim and I booked him into the hotel. All I could do for Pines was hold his hand, as it were, and listen. He was grateful as a sheepdog for the attention, all but nuzzled me with a cold wet nose.

    Do you know what the holdup is on Pines? Tim asked me to pick out a few scenes for a screen test, and I did. Nothing's happened since. Maybe you can enlighten Pines. I'm writing like mad on the Spy sequence, you'll have a dozen new pages in the morning.

Margo

Hi, Margo:

I'm scouting the Guadalupe Dunes for the desert scenery DeMille used in the 1923 movie. I've never seen this natural wonder of California before. It's gorgeous, very like the Sinai sand vistas, but with today's tourism and the new wildlife preserves, the place may not do for us. DeMille buried his colossal sets right here deep under the dunes, and there they are still! Spooky.

My office sent me your note about Pines. I can't do a screen test until I've had my face-to-face with the actor. It was scheduled for the day after he arrived. The holdup is Pines's agent. Tim's London man is buying the fellow out before he smells the Moses angle. It's all very small potatoes, and I'm sorry for the Aussie. I laughed out loud about his wet cold nose. My office faxed your script pages to me out here. Spy sequence starts off brilliantly. Keep it brisk and *please* keep God's lines short and few! God doesn't play well, He's all CGI effects at best, and the audience is on to those, especially the teenagers. We don't want God getting laughs.

Arnie

Chateau Marmont

8221 Sunset Boulevard
Hollywood, California 90046

Dear Mr. Warshaw:

I am mailing this letter from the airport, as for nearly a week I've heard nothing from you. My father needs me back home, I phoned him and he's not well. I feel badly about the money. Suppose I refund you $10,000? I did come in good faith, but I began to feel as I did in London while I'd wait for Geoff Smallweed to answer my phone calls and e-mails. I decided then I'd rather do business with the devil, so I flew home. I don't mean to offend you, but I was feeling the same way in the Chateau Marmont. Whatever went wrong, I'm sure you meant well, sending for me. Please give my best to Ms. Solovei, she was very decent to me. I hope your Moses film will be a great epic.

Sincerely

Perry Pines

From: Tim Warshaw
To: Shayna Daniels
CC: James C. Bearing, Margo, Arnold

Dear Shayna,

See the attached letter! I can't believe my eyes. That the doofus is walking off from a chance at Moses is weird enough. His offer to give back half the dough—an actor *returning* money—is like a total eclipse of the sun, only less usual. Anyway, that's that! I was clear off my head when I made you send for him. Panic in the wee hours. Jim, just drop Smallweed. One less knot in my gut.

Tim

SHIRLEY JUNG SCHARF

Dear Margo,

Guess what? I ran into Josh and that Debbie again! You remember Nechama Goodstein, our class gargoyle who made aliyah, poor thing? Well, she's back, with an Israeli hubby, handsome, a hi-tech guy, reserve army colonel. Such luck! The wedding was quite a do. I must say, for an English professor Debbie shone in the carrying on when he stamped on the glass, cavorting in the women's circle, beautiful red hair flying wildly, like her skirt. Joshua was there, watching Debbie prance around. He told me she'd just heard that her fiancé in Afghanistan was found alive!

Avram and I are planning a trip to the California national parks with the kids, so don't be too surprised if all the Scharfs fall in on the one celebrity we know, just to say we saw you!

Best regards,

Shirley

From: Smodar
To: Hezzie Jacobs

Hezzie, your Houston office is closed for some holiday. Mr. Gluck has ordered me to track you down. He's in a villa at the Beverly Hills Hotel, and you're to come there without fail by tomorrow the latest. Mr. Gluck has visited WarshaWorks and is boiling.

Smodar

Chapter Six

THE ARBITRATOR

(LETTER)

JAMES C. BEARING
BARRISTER
77 BOND STREET
LONDON W1, ENGLAND

Mr. Timothy Warshaw
WarshaWorks
Century City, CA 90067

Dear Tim:

Re: Geoffrey Smallweed

Your instruction to drop this man is easier said than done. He's an ongoing nuisance. At the outset, when I guaranteed he was no problem, he'd already accepted an offer of £5,000. He came to my office to sign the release. The cash was on my desk in thousand-pound notes. Pen in hand, he changed his mind and asked for

£7,500. Either that, he said, or the price thereafter would be fifty thousand. Of course I said no. He left, saying, "Very well, then, fifty thousand it is." Then you wrote me to drop the matter. A week or so later he returned and generously offered to settle for forty thousand pounds. At intervals since then he has been pestering my secretary, Orly, who ignores him, by stepping down his price via faxes, e-mails, phone calls, and special delivery letters. This morning came a courier with his "absolutely final offer," he would take the five thousand pounds. Are you still interested?

Jim

My major investor is on the warpath, and I have to watch not only nickels and dimes, but pennies. His laser eye would spot that expenditure in the weekly cost report and give me grief I don't need. *Forget* Smallweed, once and for all.

MARGOLIT SOLOVEI

Hi, Debbie,

Thanks for *Crotchet Castle*. I'll probably devour it in two nights as I did *Headlong Hall*. The marginal notes in your copies (which I will soon return) are incisive and amusing. I don't know how we missed Thomas Peacock in my lit major at Barnard. Myopia in the English Department, perhaps. You're right, his novels are gems of British high comedy, but as to film possibilities, doubtful. Static brilliance will lose even an art-house audience. Wilde always told a story, remember. You should go for a Ph.D. on Peacock.

I know your visits to Cy at Walter Reed must be difficult. The hospital isn't far from Joshua's house, and he looks in on Cy now and then. Under the bandages and splints, he says, Cy's the same old wild guy, raring to recover and fly again. Naturally, he's more subdued when you come and see him all bedridden and unmanned. He'll get over it. It's great that he starts to walk with a physical therapist next week. Miracle enough that he made it back! Be thankful for that, and for the excellent prognosis.

This pen pal thing of ours is the current light of my life. The *bolvans* in the film business wouldn't know Thomas Peacock from Thomas Jefferson, if they've heard of either one. The screenplay lumbers along, but the less said, the better. I'm under the gun.

All best,

Mashie

Weizmann Institute of Science
Rehovot, Israel 76100

Department of Genetics

Mr. Joshua Lewin
Lewin, Rubinstein & Curtis
1440 K Street, NW
Washington, DC 20005

Dear Mr. Lewin:

A simple matter of fact is being obfuscated by your firm. The Institute board has now approved all expenses for my traveling to Australia to confront Dr. William Gillespie. We coauthored two papers and an article in *Nature* before I made aliyah. The last thing I want, of course, is to interrupt my work for a wearisome round-trip to Australia. If I have to go, I will.

Sincerely,

Marvin E. Zivoni
Professor of Genetics

NEW YORK UNIVERSITY

Dear Mashie:

Cy walked all this week! He started with a walker, now he leans on the physical therapist's arm, a hospital staff lady. I'll try to fly down Sunday for the day. I saw the little article in the Times Arts section about casting Moses, evidently still up in the air. I couldn't last a week in that environment. More power to you.

Now, just how well do you know one Shirley Scharf? She claims you've been best friends since Bais Yaakov days, that recently you showed her and her kids around Universal Studios, and so forth. Josh was in town, he was going to dinner with her and Avram at the 57th Street kosher steak house and asked me to come. I said sure. Those huge grilled rib steaks! Afterward Josh said that you consider Shirley, forgive me if I quote, "a revolting pain in the ass." Anyway, great dinner. Josh seemed low and tired, especially when she went on and on about you.

As to Peacock, a doctorate has long been on my agenda. Strange man, strange books, intimate of Shelley, father-in-law of Meredith, East India Company bureaucrat—but don't get me started on Peacock. I think I can demonstrate a disappointed first love with facts and names (see his rueful poem "Love and Age") as a key to his "static brilliance." Needs much digging.

Fondly,

Debbie

MARGO

Dear Debbie:

Hastily (I'm called to a meeting): Shirley and I were best friends in Bais Yaakov, true enough. She was the class cat, and I enjoyed her sharp gibes about the other girls. Then we met Josh at an engagement party, both of us went ape for him, and he liked me. It's bad business to cross Shirley. Our falling-out was a bloodletting, all my blood. Still, I'm a forgiving sort. Lately she's been sending me fawning letters about the Moses project, invariably with a needle about you and Josh as an "item." She barged in on me here with her brood and her Arthur. To cut the visit short, I got her passes to Universal from my producer. I didn't show her anything but the door. Now I'm off through that door.

Warmly,

Mashie

HW Film Memo No. 9

After a quiet month or so, that film project has come crashing into my office once more. I was rolling along in Aaron's diary, describing the plague of frogs, and as I wrote I was laughing out loud. It's both frightening and funny, the way Aaron tells it. Aaron is a dry unconsciously ironic voice that *works*. My grandfather taught me about the frogs just that way, quoting comical Midrash extravagances. Anyway, a FedEx envelope came from Margo's Washington attorney, one Joshua Lewin, requesting a Skype conversation "on a matter of some urgency."

BSW surprised me. "Oh, why not? We're in this now." So it's on for noon tomorrow, PST.

FILM MEMO: LEWIN SKYPE CONFERENCE

(I recorded the talk. The picture was clearer than usual. He was sitting at a big desk with shelves of law books behind him. I was at my desktop monitor, BSW sitting offscreen. "You talk to him" were the orders. He started with pleasantries about my novels. His favorite is Inside, Outside.*)*

HW: Thank you. Mine, too.

LEWIN: I'm interrupting your creative day—

HW: I said you could. What's up?

LEWIN: An offer I'm told you can't refuse.

HW: From whom?

LEWIN: A gentleman named Hezzie Jacobs—

(Voice off) Uh-oh.

LEWIN:—approached me, speaking for Tim Warshaw.

(Voice off) UH-OH!

HW: That's Mrs. Wouk.

LEWIN: I gather. Good afternoon, Mrs. Wouk.

(Voice off) Afternoon.

LEWIN: *(rueful smile)* Is the meeting over, or shall I continue?

(BSW shows up behind me on the screen in the small window.)

BSW: Hi.

LEWIN: Hi. I need, say, five minutes to convey a murky ball of Hollywood wax.

HW: You've got five. **Go.**

(BSW moves offscreen. Lewin conveys the ball of wax pretty clearly. I'm not about to type out all that slippery financial goo. The gist: a superstar may do Moses if he's guaranteed many millions in escrow, and only Gluck can handle that. Gluck can be approached only if I'll read the incomplete screenplay, now far along, and approve it.)

(Short silence.)

(Voice off) Meeting's over.

133

LEWIN: *(wryly smiles)* Mr. Wouk?

HW: You heard my agent.

(BSW reappears behind me in the small window.)

BSW: You can't be very surprised.

LEWIN: Not very.

BSW: Why have you done this? Is Margo involved?

LEWIN: She knew. Once I was told the offer I felt I had to let you know. Wouldn't you like to hear what it was?

HW: *(I glance at BSW, who shrugs.)* Okay, what was it?

LEWIN: A percentage of box office receipts off the top.

(Only mega-superstars ask for that and rarely get it.)

BSW: *(reappears in the window)* What percentage?

LEWIN: Terms to be arranged.

BSW: I thought so. Just curious.

LEWIN: Meeting over?

HW: Clearly.

LEWIN: It's been an honor, sir. Mrs. Wouk, this glimpse of you has been a singular privilege. All my respects.

(In the small window, she smiles the smile that hooked me sixty-odd years ago.)

BSW: 'Bye.

(The screen goes blank.)

BSW: Well! As lawyers go, rather a charmer! He's good-looking.

HW: So who's the old fool now? (That's what I *thought.* I held my tongue. Good thing, too.)

MARGO

Dear Beshie:

What wonderful news! Getting married, and to a beautiful, religious Brazilian girl! That's carrying your importing business to a new level, dear brother. It took an exotic like this Fridja Najman to break through your bachelor shell. We Bais Yaakov cuties bored you. Hurray for her.

You ought to plan a honeymoon in California, at least to start with. The marvelous state parks will be all new to Fridja, and if you'll bring her to meet your breakaway sister, I'll give her the A-plus Hollywood tour.

Love to her and to you,

Mashie

JAMES C. BEARING
BARRISTER
77 BOND STREET
LONDON W1, ENGLAND

Mr. Tim Warshaw
WarshaWorks
Century City, CA 90067

Re: Geoffrey Smallweed

This morning he showed up with such a humble mien and beaten air that Orly actually brought him in to me. He pleaded wife and gambling troubles, confessed he'd been a neglectful agent, badly needed 4,000 American dollars and would settle for that and sign the release forthwith.

I earnestly advise you to accept this offer. In my experience moviemaking takes strange turns, and you never know. As I am shortly going on a cruise to Scandinavia, please expedite reply.

Sincerely,

Jim

Participants: Hezzie Jacobs
                 Timothy Warshaw
                 Arnold Granit

WARSHAW: Well, let's start. Lewin couldn't get past Wouk's wife.

JACOBS: I still say it was worth a shot—

GRANIT: Agreed, but she's a madwoman. Now, looking ahead—

WARSHAW: Wait, Arnie, one bit of business. Jim Bearing reports that Smallweed is down to four thousand dollars, and he urges that I take it. Hezzie, can you advance that?

JACOBS: Me? Four thousand? Who's Smallweed? What's it all about?

WARSHAW: Look, Hezzie, Andrea will fill you in on Smallweed. I don't want the item on our cost report. You know Gluck—

JACOBS: Well, I guess I can handle four thousand.

GRANIT: Gentleman, can I talk about Johnny Depp? I had lunch with him. He thinks my *Xenophon* is the best epic film of all time and—

JACOBS: Say! Depp could play the living bejesus out of Pharaoh.

GRANIT: Hezzie, I'm dealing with three Pharaohs right now. Pharaoh's nothing. It's Moses.

WARSHAW: He *can't* be interested?

GRANIT: We did touch on Moses, but only in passing—you know—

WARSHAW: I know the whole drill, Arnie. Smoke dreams, forget it.

(End of excerpt.)

LEWIN, RUBINSTEIN & CURTIS
1440 K Street, NW
Washington, DC 20005

Joshua Lewin, Senior Partner

Dr. Marvin Zivoni
Department of Genetics
Weizmann Institute of Science
Rehovot, Israel 76100

Re: Nullarbor Patent Infringement

Dear Dr. Zivoni:

Regarding your dispute with our client, Nullarbor Ponds, I pass on a matter of mutual interest. Dr. Adin Genakowski of Tufts gave a lecture at the Cosmos Club here the other day, "Freedom from Mideast Oil: Genetically Engineered Algae." Strange fellow, young face, bushy black whiskers, ear curls, yarmulke. I'm told that he's a coming Nobel laureate, and I can believe it. He made the altered molecules almost understand-able for the moment. In the Q&A about the venture capitalists who are betting on algae, he said big payoffs might well be ten or fifteen years down the road. I invited him to tea in the lounge. He knows about you, of course, but not Nullarbor. He earnestly advised against a lawsuit. It would take years, judges and juries would be baffled, it would just be—I quote his words—"a costly fucking crapshoot."

This from one so piously gotten up jarred me, and I taxed him on it. Secular socialist parents, he explained, no bar mitzvah. He discovered Yiddishkeit at Harvard in a Jewish eating house. Evidently he has gone all the way and then some. About our dispute, he may have a point. Would he be acceptable to the institute in an arbitration? We exchanged cards.

Best,

Joshua Lewin

SHIRLEY JUNG SCHARF

Dear Margo:

Guess what, Avram and I went to DC to look into a real estate deal, and we visited Joshua's friend, Cy Diamond, at Walter Reed Hospital. Cy was walking in a corridor, leaning on the physical therapist. His face is half-bandaged and he limps with a cast on his left leg. He seemed sort of foggy. I explained that we'd had dinner recently with his fiancée Deborah and Josh. Actually, Arthur took him into a real estate syndicate two years ago, but since it went sort of sour we didn't bring this up. The therapist bowled me over! So help me, she looks like Grace Kelly, all creamy white and blonde. I think we interrupted their conversation. She got sort of snappish when I explained that in our religion visiting the sick is a mitzvah. Tell Debbie Kamaiko to keep an eye on that therapist! Word to the wise. No mental match for an English professor, maybe, but wow!

Well, I hope that by now Mr. Granit has found a Moses. I can't wait to see who it'll be. If only Henry Fonda were still alive!

Sincerely,

Shirley

MARGOLIT SOLOVEI ENTERPRISES LLC
10235 SUNSET BOULEVARD
LOS ANGELES, CA 90077

Mr. Perry Pines
Crooked Creek Farm
RMB 6432, Timboon
Victoria, Australia 3268

Dear Perry:

This letter will come as a surprise I'm sure. No doubt you've read or heard that WarshaWorks has as yet failed to find a Moses. Ever since our drink in the Chateau Marmont bar, when I write lines for Moses, I've been hearing and picturing you. Call it a hunch! As the Torah says somewhere, "Moses was the humblest man on earth." You're that sort of man, humble yet a powerhouse. I was so proud of the way you walked out on Tim Warshaw! Your offer to refund half your expense money astounded every-one, yet it was just like you. Warshaw might even have taken it, he's watching the pennies, but Mr. Granit laughed him out of it.

144

My purpose in writing is to urge you to consider coming back here for a screen test that you will get, *I promise I'll see to it!* I'll anxiously await your reply, meantime drudging on, putting words in your mouth as Moses. I can't help it.

Sincerely,

Margo Solovei

From: Dr. Marvin Zivoni
To: Joshua Lewin

Adin Genakowski is a top geneticist, if slightly cuckoo. He's well-known and admired in Israel, and would carry weight in an arbitration.

From: Margo
To: Arnold Granit and Tim Warshaw

Tim, Arnold, it's imperative we meet today in Arnold's office to reconsider Perry Pines.

Chapter Seven

THE SCREEN TEST

(MEMO)

From the desk of

Arnold Granit

(Dictated from my Death Valley unit but not read)

Tim,

You handled Margo admirably yesterday. The notion of casting Pines is utterly off the wall, we both know that. Of course the guy's willing to come back for the test, why shouldn't he be? Margo has a case on him, no other way to explain it. I have this epic undertaking under firm control, most of my old staff have rallied around, but the whole thing rests on two unsteady pillars, Margo's productivity and Gluck's health. So bravo for ending the meeting with "I'll think about it"! Had you turned her down cold, she'd have been quite capable of blowing her top and ceasing to write, flying off to Acapulco or Majorca or God knows where. Which would be calamitous in our damnable race against time. Let's keep Margo writing *and* keep Pines among his sheep! Maybe no actor can rise to the stature of Moses, but we still have to get a grand figure, not a lunkhead Aussie bit player.

Arnold

Sackler School
of Graduate Biomedical Research
Tufts University
Boston, MA 02111

Professor Adin Genakowski

Professor Marvin E. Zivoni
Department of Genetics
Weizmann Institute of Science
Rehovot, Israel 76100

Hi, Marvin:

Recently I encountered Mr. Joshua Lewin at the Cosmos Club in Washington, where I lectured on algae versus Middle East oil. We talked quite a bit about your dispute with Professor Gillespie. Lewin doesn't pretend to understand the genetics, and I strongly advised him against going to court. The law hasn't caught up to the science, I pointed out, one simply ends up with experts testifying on both sides, just a crapshoot. In fact, I called it a "costly fucking crapshoot," which sort of pinned back his ears. My former undergraduate locutions slip out now and then.

I know Gillespie well, of course. How on earth did you and he get involved over algae ponds in the Australian outback, anyhow?

Cheers,

Adin

From the desk of

Arnold Granit

Margo—

I hope you're enjoying your Catalina Island cottage. Great idea, inspiring place to work. Tim and I can't wait to hear you read your "Rock II" sequence. Your promise to bring it in Monday has us agog. Shayna Daniels is flying in for it. About Perry Pines, we both take your word that he seems right to you, but on reflection neither Tim nor I can see him in the part, and Tim won't pay for his travel. Old man Gluck's uncanny eye for odd small expenditures has Tim on edge. Sorry! You're doing a magnificent job now with the script, I'm starting to sense we have a winner here, keep up the good work!

Arnold

Bernard Solovei, Importer

1230 Main Street

Passaic, New Jersey 07055

Dear Mashie:

Well, the wedding day is set, June 5th in São Paulo. Her father flew up from São Paulo to meet with Tatti, and they really hit it off. He's a sweet man, speaks only Portuguese (besides, of course, Yiddish, old country Russian, Rabbinic Hebrew, and Ivrit). Imagine! He'll send his private plane for Tatti and Mommy—you too if you can come —*and Tatti will officiate at the wedding,* how about that? Fridja loves your notion of a California honeymoon. She's dying to meet you and see everything in Hollywood. Wait till you meet her!

Love,

Beshie

Weizmann Institute of Science
Rehovot, Israel 76100

Department of Genetics

Professor Adin Genakowski
Sackler School of Graduate Biomedical
  Research
Tufts University
Boston, MA 02111

Dear Adin:

It's quite a story, the Nullarbor Ponds. When you brought your Harvard alumni group here you surely met our finance chairman, Mayer Shisgall. Mayer would never miss a shot at some Harvard Jews. Mayer circles the world, talking at temples, synagogues, men's clubs, ladies' sister-hoods, he's not here half the time but he sure rakes in the dough for Israeli science. You'll remember him, a short, fast-talking man with flying wings of wavy blond hair, and a twinkling eye.

Well, on Mayer's last whirl through Sydney and Melbourne, he heard that Perth now has 7,000

Jews, so he flew out to have a go at them, and came back on the train through the outback that stops at Nullarbor, for tourists to watch the whales and see the algae ponds. Mayer knows all about my project, and on a hunch he brought back a sample of the pond water, and there were my molecules, no question of it, and Mayer alerted our legal department, hence the spate of lawyer letters, all Mayer's doing. I'm trying to stay out of all that.

Look, why not come back here one day to lecture? I can wangle you an invitation, all expenses paid and a hefty honorarium.

All best,

Marvin

GRANIT PRODUCTIONS
10 CENTURY PLAZA
CENTURY CITY, CA 90067

Script Conference: Rock II Sequence

Present: Solovei, Warshaw, Granit, Jacobs,
            Daniels
Agenda: Rock II sequence, reading by
            Margo Solovei
Recording: Andrea

Margo's reading timed out at 10½ minutes, followed by a long silence.

WARSHAW: *(almost in a whisper)* Awesome.
JACOBS: You're writing way over your head, Margo.
DANIELS: Astounding. It works, truly works.
JACOBS: This film, I predict, will outgross *King Kong*. What am I saying? All three *King Kongs*—
GRANIT: Well done, Margo.
MARGO: *(near tears)* Oh, thank you, Arnie, dear! Thank you all. It's written in heart's blood, that I can tell you.

GRANIT: Yes, very well done. Only, to be frank, I don't quite get it.

WARSHAW: Don't get *what,* Arnie?

GRANIT: Why Moses and Aaron got punished so harshly. Never to enter the Promised Land! What did they do that was so terrible?

JACOBS: Arnie, baby, they disobeyed God. Like Adam and Eve.

GRANIT: How you talk! Where's your snake? Where's your apple? God told Moses and Aaron to assemble the people and get water out of a rock, same as he did in the desert forty years before. And Moses did it and got the water, same as before—

DANIELS: You weren't listening, Arnold. This time God told them to go and *talk* to the rock. Moses *hit* the rock.

GRANIT: I was too listening. God also told Moses *to take the stick with him.* To do what? Chase the livestock away from the rock? Okay, so Moses *hit* the rock. Big deal! For that he and Aaron couldn't cross the Jordan into the Holy Land? Pardon me, folks, God as nitpicker won't play—

(Confusion of comments, everyone talking at once to Arnold Granit except Margo. When they stop, she speaks.)

MARGO: Arnie, you really grasped my scene. Only you.

(More confused talking at once.)

MARGO: *(over the babble)* LET ME SAY SOMETHING!

(Silence.)

MARGO: That's the exact question I asked my father when I was nine, and starting to think! Tatti—that's my father—gave me a big hairy kiss, all excited at my sharpness. He ran to a shelf and pulled down a fat Book of Numbers full of commentaries, to show me how his favorite commentator, Or ha-Hayyim, that's Light of Life, quotes ten different reasons that ten previous authorities gave why Moses and Aaron were punished.[1] Sure enough, old Light of Life disagrees with all ten, then gives his own reason. "See?" says Tatti joyously. "*There's* your answer, Mashie. Oh, the holy Light of Life! Such a giant, such an uprooter of mountains!" Well, I thought Light of Life's answer was no more convincing than the others, but having scored a kiss, I precociously shut up. Nice going, Arnie.

GRANIT: Why, thanks, Margo. Do I get a kiss?

(Laughter.)

MARGO: Don't press your luck. You're not nine years old.

(More laughter.)

GRANIT: Shucks, no kiss. So what's the actual answer?

---

1. Ohr ha-Chaim, Rabbi Chaim Ben Atar, 1696–1743. (No English translation yet exists.)—HW, 2011

SPEAKERPHONE CLICKS ON: Mr. Granit—

GRANIT: I *told* you, Christina, no interruptions!

SPEAKERPHONE: Sir, it's for Margo, emergency call—

MARGO: Emergency? For *me?*

SPEAKERPHONE: It's the desk clerk in your Catalina hotel, Margo, he's panicky, almost like calling nine-one-one—

MARGO: Put him on. . . . Stanley, what's up?

SPEAKERPHONE: Ma'am, I'm calling from the manager's office. There's this fellow at the desk, very rude, won't give me his name, demands the number of your cottage—a huge hulking guy, strange accent, getting unruly. Oh, Lord, now he's coming in here! Sir, sir, this office is private *(different, very deep voice)*. Is that Margolit Solovei? Let me talk to her!

DANIELS: Holy cow, it's Mr. Penis . . .

SPEAKERPHONE: Ms. Solovei, *Daily Variety* says you're working at this hotel now. I thought I'd surprise you—

MARGO: Well, you goddamn have—!

GRANIT: *(loud groan)* Call the cops. Have him thrown off Catalina.

WARSHAW: With an anchor around his neck—

MARGO: Look, Mr. Pines, I'm in a conference. There's a helicopter to Catalina, I'll be there soon, take a walk on the beach, or something—

SPEAKERPHONE: Heck, I'll meet you at the helipad—

MARGO: Good enough. 'Bye—Christina, get me on the next flight—

SPEAKERPHONE: Will do.

MARGO: Of all the total rattlebrains!

WARSHAW: You weren't expecting the man?

GRANIT: The truth, now, Margo!

MARGO: I'm flabbergasted! Thanks for your marvelous comments, everyone! Now I can blaze through the last few sequences. I'm going right back to work this afternoon—

GRANIT: What'll you do about him?

MARGO: Oh, yes, him. . . . Look, Tim, book him into the Chateau Marmont for now, will you? Talk to you later. 'Bye, all.

(Margo leaves.)

GRANIT: She's all in a flutter. She sent for him.

JACOBS: Say, I'd like to meet this character—

DANIELS: Well, well! I flew here from Turkey just to hear that Rock II scene. It was worth it! My vote is, give Mr. Penis his screen test already! A nice hunk he is, but Moses he ain't. Best way to get rid of him.

GRANIT: By God, Shayna, maybe so, at that.

(End of minutes.)

Moses Film Memo

8:30 a.m.

The film thing again! Margo asked us to an "important" Moses screen test, so we went. When we arrived, Granit was telling Warshaw and Ziegler that he had some interesting CGI footage for the Red Sea crossing. The screening room went dark and, lo, we were in a typhoon, mountainous waves roaring and crashing, howl and screech of Force 12 winds all around us. Bone-shaking stuff! I have a traumatic horror of high winds ever since the *Southard* was wrecked in a typhoon at Okinawa. I sat there white-knuckled, as a red dawn slowly brightened over a vast sandbar that emerged from the waves, and a shadowy horde came marching out across the sand. "They're still playing with it, of course," Granit said, as the lights came up. "It's strictly Scriptural. The Bible says that a mighty east wind blew the whole night before they crossed—"

Mr. Gluck rolled in, foot up on a board, pushed by Ishmael and followed by Jacobs. Margo scampered to kiss the old mogul, told him the actor was in an anteroom, too nervous to watch the test, and he'd come in afterward. "He's an Aussie like you," she said. "His name's Perry Pines. I should warn you, this is a crude preliminary test—"

"Nu, nu," said Gluck, Yiddish for "get on with it," and Ishmael lifted him into an armchair.

Crude indeed it was. Green screen, actor in travel clothes, no makeup, Margo's voice off-screen feeding him cue lines both as God and Pharaoh, a decidedly unhelpful effect. This Pines is a huge fellow with a square open face and a mop of sandy hair. One had to imagine him robed and bearded. Short test, three passages from Exodus: the Burning Bush scene, the face-off with Pharaoh and his court over the locusts, and his last farewell to Pharaoh. Pines delivered the qualms and self-doubts of Moses at the Burning Bush well enough, but tearing loose against Pharaoh about the locusts he was another man—I'd say another actor. And when he thundered Moses' last words to Pharaoh: *Thus says the Lord, toward midnight I will go out into the midst of the Egyptians, and every firstborn in the land of Egypt shall die, from the son of Pharaoh, who sits on the throne to the firstborn of the slave girl who is behind the millstones . . . and there shall be a great cry throughout all the land of Egypt—* so help me, the hair on my head prickled. Even BSW muttered, "Not all that bad." Then it was over, and we were all blinking in the light. Gluck said aloud, *"Aber das IST Moishe Rabenu.* Now I want to meet the actor."

Margo brought Pines in, dressed in the clothes he had worn for the test. As they shook hands, Gluck said, in his odd Aussie-Jewish accent, "So, mate, you think you can play Moses, do you?" The actor blinked and grinned at the slang greeting. "Well, mate," he shot back, "if they want me, I can sure try," and ducked into the anteroom.

Gluck laughed. "Now we go." Ishmael put him back into the wheelchair and they left. As the door closed, Warshaw exclaimed, "What the Christ did Gluck say in Yiddish?"

Margo exulted, *"But that's Moses our Teacher!"*

Granit said, "Well, he should live so long. He's an investor, not a casting director. The lummox is *out* at last, obviously, and good riddance."

"Isn't that a snap judgment, Arnie?" said Margo.

"The fact is," Jacobs put in, "the bozo sort of reminded me of Marlon Brando—"

"Brando?!" Granit choked. *"Brando?"*

"Oh, come on, Hezzie," Warshaw said, "sure you don't mean Laurence Olivier?" He turned to us. "What do you think?"

I glanced at BSW. "I think we go too," she said.

In the limo she opined that Margo was clearly hot for the Aussie as Moses but none of the others were. Jacobs just wanted to have his money back. As for Gluck, his reaction was naive, BSW thinks. Those Torah words spoken aloud by an actor moved him, nothing more. I told her that I was moved, too. "Oh, you," she said, and fell asleep for the whole ride back to Palm Springs.

I think it may come down to considering Pines after all and giving him (as *Time* joked) a Scarlett O'Hara buildup. Warshaw is desperate to start filming. No actor can do Moses, anyway, and Moneybags did say Pines was Moishe Rabenu. He who pays the piper—

Enough, enough! Beyond control, beyond concern! I lost a day on my book, when it's taking off for sure. Back to work at daylight tomorrow.

SHIRLEY JUNG SCHARF

Dear Margo,

What is happening with your Moses production? I Google it every day, and for weeks there's been nothing really new, just the same old publicity stuff, not a word about Moses. I hope the film hasn't been aborted! Hollywood is such a treacherous place, isn't it?

Did I mention that when we were in Washington, Avram picked up a bargain real estate parcel, an old building near Dupont Circle that he can renovate? He's been spending much time in DC ever since, and he keeps running into Josh and Debbie Kamaiko at Maxim's, the only kosher eating place in town. (It seems funny to call a glatt kosher place Maxim's, but the chef there is really Maxim Feitelbaum, a genuine Frenchman.) Avram always says hello to the duo—it's a small place—and they seem uncomfortable or embarrassed.

Could be his imagination? Have you heard from either of them lately, and is there any news about Cy's condition? I wonder how the professor can get away from NYU so often, but that's none of my business. Avram says he hasn't gone back to the hospital because that therapist acted so hostile.

I know you and Josh are sort of in touch lately, and I do hope something will finally come of it! None of us is getting any younger, dear, after all.

As ever,

Shirley

From: Adin Genakowski
To: Marvin Zivoni
Subject: Weizmann Institute lecture

Sure, I'd love a solo jaunt to Israel, all expenses paid plus honorarium, and of course to meet your *frum* wife. Has she got a nice sister? God was right about Adam: for a man to live alone is not good. I can't spare a rib. Fall semester, earliest?

Adin

From: Debbie
To: Margo

In haste, Friday afternoon finds me rushing through a pile of term papers. Yesterday I visited Cy and had dinner with Josh in the local kosher restaurant. Avram Scharf was there again, he often is these days. He came over to our table and said with a sly grin, "Shirley sends her regards to you two." So I assume you've been hearing from Shirley, God knows to what effect! I'm compelled to write you a long confidential e-mail. I'll do it Sunday.

Shabbat shalom,

Debbie

Crooked Creek Farm

RMB 6432, Timboon
Victoria, Australia 3268

Dear Ms. Solovei:

Thanks for your frank letter about how the test went. Please forget about my travel expenses, I had money left over from my last trip. I wouldn't have missed this experience for anything. It was a great challenge and wonderful fun trying to bring those glorious lines to life. Now that it's over, well, that's that! I'd be a fool to nurse any high hopes. Mr. Granit is quite right to test other unknown actors now for a "Plan B Moses," while still seeking an available superstar. Unlike most actors, I have a whole other life that absorbs me. Here we're in the lambing season, and I wish you could see the hundreds and hundreds of little white lambs leaping and dancing all over the farm. I think you'd understand me better. Mr. Granit is a famous director, and knows what he's doing.

My father, incidentally, got hold of an old DVD of your movie *The Unbearable Bassington*, and really liked it. You'd like him, though I guess you'll never meet. Different worlds.

Sincerely,

Perry Pines

Chapter Eight
BETWEEN US GIRLS

(E-MAIL)

From: Deborah Kamaiko
To: Margolit Solovei
Subject: Maxim's, etc.

Dearest Margo:

Herewith the confidential e-mail I promised you. I gather Shirley reported, no doubt with sledge-hammer hints of something going on, that Avram's been seeing me and Josh eating at Maxim's. Something's going on, all right, but it's between Cy and his physical therapist, not Josh and me.

Her name is Else Hviesten, quite pretty, if on the beefy side. At first she seemed strictly professional, now I'm all in knots about her. A few weeks ago when I flew to visit Cy, New York was bright and sunny, Washington was pouring rain. No umbrella, fighting for a taxi, I showed up in Cy's room a bedraggled mess. There was Hviesten, bandbox neat and quite at her ease in his bedside chair, both of them merrily laughing.

The other bed, usually occupied by a cheerful black veteran almost killed by an IED, was rumpled and empty. Something in the way she jumped up, gave me a quick arid smile and walked out, and in Cy's forced-funny greeting, "Hi there, you drowned rat," grated on me. All the way back on the shuttle I fumed.

The next time I came she was walking with him on another floor, and left him with me in a foyer for visitors, saying curtly that she'd be back to get him in fifteen minutes. We drank coffee off in a corner, and I said something about Hviesten. Cy fired up, "Why are you getting so possessive?" I fired back, "Why are you getting so defensive?" and so on and on and on, a red-hot fight in low tones. I know, I know we're both exasperated at all that's gone wrong, that he's been through hell and I haven't, that I thank God he's back, so let's say it was 90% my fault. Now about the remaining 10%. Cy's call-up by the air reserve was an unnerving jolt. We were crazily in love, we'd just become engaged, and all at once he was off to fly helicopters in the war! The night before he left for Afghanistan we spent in a hotel room, where I cast off my Bais Yaakov upbringing with my last stitch. First and only time. How did I know I'd ever see him again? How could I refuse him anything? I'll not dwell on that, I don't have to. Not to you.

Back to the present: next time I came to Walter Reed, Cy was in bed, so was his roommate, no sign of Hviesten. We couldn't really talk. I sort of apologized and he sort of accepted, but that visit was a painful fiasco. Afterward, in a deep black mood, I phoned Josh from the shuttle waiting room, and he drove right out there to join me for tuna sandwiches and sympathy. Since then, when he's free, he sometimes picks me up at Cy's hospital room and we go on to Maxim's. Josh is a kind, patient listener. He thinks I'm just badly overwrought, and he's absolutely sure there's nothing on with Cy and Hviesten. He doesn't like her either, says he finds her sly and too zaftig. Maybe that's just talk to cheer me up, but in my state it helps. And that's the story of the sightings at Maxim's.

Josh hardly talks about you, but from the little he's disclosed I'm astonished, in fact incredulous. Such unshakable one-sided devotion through so many years one finds only in Thackeray novels nowadays. You're to be envied. To be quite candid I don't understand you at all, but that's your story. Now you know mine.

Affectionate best,

Debbie

Sackler School
of Graduate Biomedical Research
Tufts University
Boston, MA 02111

Professor Adin Genakowski

Professor Marvin E. Zivoni
Department of Genetics
Weizmann Institute of Science
Rehovot, Israel 76100

Dear Marvin:

I accept the invitation to deliver the annual Hecht Lecture. It is an honor and the emolument is princely. Please thank the trustees for thinking of me.

I've been in touch with Dr. Gillespie. The legal folderol should end between you two! I am willing to go to Australia with you straight from the Hecht Lecture to thrash the matter out. Gillespie isn't adamant, he honestly thinks he's right on the molecules. Australia is a long drag nowadays, even on this shrunken crab apple of a planet, but I'd do it to make peace between two scientists I admire.

All best,

Adin

MARGO

Dear Perry Pines:

Your stouthearted letter about the screen test just got here. Snail mail takes days to reach Catalina, from Australia even more so.

Oh, those newborn white lambs, leaping and dancing by the hundreds all over your farm, they tell me so much about your other life! I continue to see you as Moses day by day, as I work on like fury to finish up the screenplay. In Yiddish mensch means a good man, and for me that's Moses, a good man— but just a man—called by God to teach his fellowmen for all time. You're a mensch, Perry—that's what old Mr. Gluck saw and heard. Don't resign yourself yet to being dropped. <u>Wait</u>. Unlike most actors, you're not hanging on a telephone call from a producer or agent. How lucky you are!

I'm delighted that my little <u>Bassington</u> film reached your dad and amused him. Maybe we'll actually meet one day. If we do, I hope it's in lambing time on Crooked Creek Farm.

Best,

Margo Solovei

GRANIT PRODUCTIONS
10 CENTURY PLAZA
CENTURY CITY, CA 90067

Dear Tim:

About Pines: your long letter meant to soft-soap me only infuriates me. Your argument is obvious and ugly. True, Gluck guaranteed that once you make *The Lawgiver*, however it turns out, he will invest $400 million-plus in WarshaWorks. Also true, even if at $160 million the movie is a dud, WarshaWorks ends up way in the black. *Therefore,* get the cameras rolling already, and *therefore,* since the old mogul likes Pines, go with Pines, QED!

This shortsighted greedy equation ignores the backbreaking work I've been doing for nearly a year to create a great movie. A dolt playing Moses will be a black hole into which all will collapse. I took on the job because Margo was my protégée. Now it possesses me. She has amazed me with the speed and quality of her screenwriting. My old staff has rallied around, the preproduction schedule goes apace, and I swear this movie can be a landmark film. To the critics I'm an old-fashioned relic, and I mean to steamroller them flat. I can't do it with Pines. I've already tested unknowns better than Pines. If you're in a panic on time, I can commit to production right now and start shooting around the Moses scenes with the pages Margo has already written, they're most of the show. If you're adamant to go with Pines, get yourself another producer. I'm out.

Arnold

From: Margo Solovei
To: Deborah Kamaiko
Subject: Sightings, etc.

Dearest Debbie:

Well, I have to laugh at poor Shirley's sightings that keep having an inside-out effect. What first linked you and me was her report of the "sexy kosher redhead" with Josh at *Hamlet,* and now her flash about Maxim's has struck from you a beautiful poignant letter, a startling confidence, and an urge in me to reciprocate. Here's what I can tell you about Josh's "one-sided devotion," which I don't fully understand either. You've read the Shaw/Terry letters, I'm sure, great playwright and great actress who never met, pouring out intense confidences on paper, which they wouldn't have touched on face-to-face. In our small way, something like that seems to be going on here.

He and I broke up over the religion. Until I met him I was the most *frum* girl in Passaic's Bais Yaakov. Tatti didn't approve of Y.U. boys, too free and modern. Neither did I. Josh shocked me from the first with his skeptical ideas and lax conduct. He dragged me into a "kosher-style" deli, for instance, and ordered tuna sandwiches for us both. By myself at the time I wouldn't have drunk a glass of water in such a *treyf* place. I choked on my first bite, got rid of it in my napkin, and just sat there while he cheerily devoured his sandwich. But I kept seeing him. Once we met at that engage-ment party, I was *gone* on him. Maybe I still am, somewhere way down in my unreachable subconscious, and if so he knows it or senses it. Is that what is at the bottom of his "devotion," which I've given up trying to fathom or discourage? When Shirley wrote me about the *Hamlet* sighting, I was both relieved and jealous. "Good! He's found somebody at last," I thought, "and I'm really free of him." Simultaneously I thought, "Pooh, that redhead, just another Bais Yaakov yenta, no competition." That makes no sense, I know. It's just the plain truth.

It was Josh, you see, who first opened my mind and cut me loose from Tatti, even before I left Passaic. We were *always* fighting over issues of observance and faith. Trouble was, he had eye-opening books to feed me, and I could only take a fierce stand on strict tradition or nothing. He was learned, he was a believer, he observed the Sabbath at all points, he could argue rings around me. I couldn't ever take the one sure way to prevail, by telling him to get lost. Like you, I won't dwell on what went on between us once I went to New York and got into Barnard. We had hot fights about religion, spaced with hot encounters of another sort indeed. We never quite made it into a hotel room, no, but then we never had a wartime parting like yours to precipitate it.

The books didn't matter at first. I'd been an obsessive reader of "outside" books in my teens, I'd devoured the old ones, *Anna Karenina*, *An American Tragedy*, also the newer Hemingways and Faulkners and such. The first books Josh tried on me, Nietzsche and Bertrand Russell, bored me, but then he hit me with Thorstein Veblen. *The Theory of the Leisure Class* shook my foundations. It's years since I've thought about such things, but one unforgettable chapter, "The Belief in Luck," is mighty hard on God. When I openly broke away from Tatti over the staff that turns into a snake, I'd read that chapter the week before.

Alas, poor Josh, talk about unintended consequences! When I dropped the religion, I really dropped it. Leaving Passaic made it easy. New environment, new friends, there was only Josh starting law school, both of us preoccupied, not seeing that much of each other. He was shocked to the bones because I went to a Broadway opening on Kol Nidre night. We had a thundering argument about it, nearly all the noise on his part. He tried reproving me, cajoling me, reeducating me. He became very angry. "You're throwing out the baby with the bathwater. You'll never forget your upbringing," he shouted, clearly appalled at what he'd wrought and feeling guilty, "you'll come back to it." I stayed calm. I *felt* calm. He had helped me to find myself. "I heard you the first time," I told him.

Well, Debbie, how will all this strike you? To me, there are believers and non-believers. I'm a well-trained, well-informed unbeliever. It will never change. That's the standoff between Josh and me. He cut my cord to Tatti, but sooner or later it would have frayed and broken.

My Lord, it's past two a.m. out here in Catalina. There's a low yellow moon making a path across the water to my window. I'm light-headed from lack of sleep, working till midnight on my screenplay. I started this letter to cool down, and instead I'm in overdrive. I can't stop till I've told you this, though I may delete it in the morning. The afternoon I left Passaic, Tatti and I had a last sad talk in his study, where he was poring over a Bobover volume. He was kind and resigned. His farewell in Yiddish, as I came into the room, was this: "So, Mashie, I'm losing you. God runs the world. One thing I can tell you. You leave me a *bsulah*,[1] and you'll return to me a *bsulah*." It shook me up, though I tried to make light of it. "Is that a blessing, Tatti, or a curse?" "It's the truth, my child," he said. "Go in health."

So anyway . . . about that therapist and Cy, something tells me Josh is right. He usually is. After all, walking with Cy all that time, holding him close, she had to get a bit chummy with him, at least. For his part, a pretty woman likes him—so what? Let it go at that, and keep eating with Josh

---

1. Maiden, virgin.—HW

at Maxim's. It's good for you both. I don't know about Josh's women, if any, and I don't want to, but a sexy kosher redhead is just the thing for keeping him my Josh . . . there, it slipped out.

Delete? Send? Well, the hell with it, neither right now. Oh, Debbie, Tatti's piercing parting words! Oh, this crummy Vanity Fair of a town where I live and work! The whisper is rife among the guys that I'm a lesbian or something. Their male egos can't grasp that one man once set the bar so high, peacocks can't fly over it. I swear I'm maundering with fatigue; this is nobody else's business, not even my darling Debbie's. DELETE! DELETE! Sure, sure, in the morning. Night-night.

Mashie

From: Deborah Kamaiko
To: Margolit Solovei
Subject: YOU WON'T BELIEVE THIS!

Margo, *Margo,* MARGO!

I've just discarded a long handwritten letter, heavy burbling about you and me, Bais Yaakov, sex, Josh, the religion, whatnot, it all at once seems so stupid and out of date! *Margo, Else Hviesten has run off with Avram Scharf! So help me God!* I'm at home, I've been dancing around my room like a maniac, the fact is I tripped over my poor cat, Emerson, he was so frightened by my antics he ran in circles, tangled my feet, and bang, down I went to a yowl, yowl, yowl, Emerson doing his bagpipes cussing at me. Nothing serious, nobody hurt, everything's great . . .

All I know so far is what Cy told me over the phone a few minutes ago, both of us laughing like two kids high on pot, laughing at ourselves, and at the huge surprise, and, I'm afraid, at poor Shirley, who has my sympathy. It seems that when they came to Walter Reed to wish Cy a *refuah shlema*, Avram was madly smitten with

185

Else at sight, got in touch with her on the q.t., never had a big real estate deal in DC. It was all nonsense, a cover story for his frequent trips to Washington to woo her. I guess it took some wooing, it's been a while, but now—WOO-WOO! Forgive me, dearest Margo, I'm shouting down at you from Cloud Nine.

As for you, Josh, and the peacocks out there, I have a lot to say but not now, I'm too dizzy with relief. In a word, my basic reaction is *screw* Thorstein Veblen! Time for Miss Ambitious Auteur to get on with her life! You've made your unbeliever point to yourself, your Tatti, your Joshua, and me, and I'll just SEND this before I have time to regret being so smarty-pants with an artist so far above and beyond me, the most accomplished woman I know (although, like Ellen Terry, only on paper so far).

Forever yours,

The Kosher Redhead

From the desk of

TIM WARSHAW

Margo, where are you, and are you all right? It's almost noon. You're not in your office at Universal, your Melrose Ave. apartment doesn't answer, your cottage in Catalina doesn't answer, and your moronic desk clerk won't bang at your door as I pleaded. I sent you a perturbed urgent e-mail this morning. Arnie told me yesterday afternoon he was going to Catalina to hear you read a new scene to him, and this morning he showed up in my office, to say I'm to join him at 3 P.M. for another look at the Pines screen test! Something went on between you and Arnie last night. I need your input or I'll be utterly in the dark. I'm sending this fax to all your locations. CALL me the moment you get it, or I'll be hopping the helo for Catalina myself.

MARGO

Sorry about being incommunicado, Tim. Woke early and walked seven miles on the beach after coffee, thinking and thinking about Arnie's visit and stuff. Herewith, a copy of my typed-up shorthand notes made after Arnie's visit. I keep steno pads on all my work, always have, learned Gregg at college to eat, got the habit of using it for notions of plays, also notes during rehearsals and conferences. Simplest way to fill you in, though some details are very personal. Please shred the copy once you've read it! See you at three, I'm coming in.

M.

Arnie, Baal Peor Scene

Whole scene out!

Second sex orgy comes too late in movie . . . need something else, before Moses climbs Mount Nebo. . . . Deut's mostly a recap of desert wanderings, I remind him . . . and of laws, starting with the Sh'ma, "Hear O Israel . . ." etc., . . . Arnie lights up. learned Sh'ma in Sunday school . . . repeats it in stumbling Hebrew, delighted with himself . . . poor Arnie —thought God said it, not Moses . . .

Ad-libbing . . . sort of farewell Sermon on Mount Nebo . . . strong quotes from Deut . . . big actor's aria for Moses to assembled multitude . . . Arnie gets all worked up, "That's it, that's IT!" Says even Pines sounded good with Scripture words.

Martinis, watching setting sun on patio, arguing about screen test. . . . On second martini Arnie barks, "Come on, admit it, you're besotted with that Aussie muscleman." *BESOTTED!* . . . Laughing and laughing at him . . . remind him of "sheepdog with cold, wet nose." He grudgingly laughs . . . we both laugh like hell. . . . Ice broken!

Room service steaks, wine . . . Arnie drinks lots of wine . . . glorious wife. . . . Blockbuster *Xenophon* all her idea . . . got him to read *Anabasis*, great classic. . . . Told him a bit about Josh . . . verges on soft, intimate evening . . . bit of trouble shooing the old dear out . . . kiss or two . . . or three or four. . . . He left cheered up, will look again at Pines' test first thing.

SHIRLEY JUNG SCHARF

Dear Margo:

You must have heard by now from Professor Kamaiko that my poor fish of a husband got hooked by that unspeakable pseudo–Grace Kelly "therapist," and they're both off and away together! I want you to know my side. It's not an end, it's a beginning, and when I'm through with Avram I hope he packed his bags well, because he'll own nothing else, no property, no credit cards, no bank accounts, no nothing. I'm in the process of filleting him good and proper, believe you me. She'll be left with a fish bone, and I hope it sticks in her throat and chokes her. Long ago, when he and I had our first fights, I found the best divorce lawyer in Manhattan, just in case. They call him Junkyard Dog Janeway, and he's already swung into action like a first responder.

Well, I had to unburden my heart. You're my best friend in the world, I still remember how you showed us around Hollywood. I hope by now you have your Moses and it'll all turn out fine. To think that Josh and that futile sneak who fathered my kids were once buddies! Avram's father knew him well enough to tie up every building he thinks he owns, either with me or one of the kids. Avram never looked into the contracts his father gave him to sign. They're flying to her hometown, Trondheim. I had to Google Trondheim, something went on there in World War II between the Nazis and the Brits, but nothing like what will go on between Junkyard Dog Janeway and any Norwegian ambulance chaser who will take Avram's case on spec. I was a perfect wife to Avram for fifteen years, and now I'm sitting pretty and she's welcome to that two-faced penniless limp bastard!

Sincerely,

Shirley

Hezzie, regarding your request for comment on latest Nullarbor Investors Report, Mr. Gluck in hospital & unavailable.

From: Hezzie Jacobs
To: Tim Warshaw, Arnold Granit

Dear Tim and Arnold:

Nix to your new request for another pre-production advance, don't you know that Louie Gluck is in Emanuel Hospital in Melbourne, "incommunicado"? I phoned Smodar, pestered her at length about his condition, not a word more out of her. *When will screenplay be finished for Wouk approval?*

Hezzie

Film Memo No. 13: Granit Turnabout

Well, good-bye to *Aaron's Diary* for now. Arnold Granit phoned. Crisis! Louis Gluck is in a hospital in Melbourne, unreachable, for all anyone knows at death's door. Solovei's script is nearly done, just one or two more sequences. Startling news, they're going with Perry Pines!

Granit exacted from me a promise to read the script right away. He was dead sure I'd approve it. It came by messenger. I was leafing through the pages when BSW showed up, looking elegant in a fresh hairdo, saw the script, froze, and pointed like a hunting dog, "What is *that?*" She jammed on her agent's hat and gave me the works. "All right, you said you'd read the thing, so read it, return it without comment, and get back to *Aaron's Diary!*" A hard woman with that hat on.

Now came the kicker. I was actually writing this note when the computer goes whoop-whoop and who comes up on Skype but Louie Gluck! First time he's ever called me. So he can do Skype, and from the hospital yet! Picture of health, he's sitting up in bed, halfway around the planet. A nurse is serving him tea. "Hello there," he says.

"Why, hello. I'm amazed. You're okay?"

196

"*Baruch Hashem.* Passed my annual physical with flying colors. After the exam I always relax for a week in this hospital to recharge my batteries. I endowed it. Tell you why I'm calling. Don't approve that incomplete script."

"Good Lord, how do you know about it? You're incommunicado, I was told—"

"Well, I know. Just remind those Hollywood *drayers*[2] once more that a contract is a contract."

"You, too? That's what my wife told me."

"Great woman. Listen to her. My best to her." He waves and smiles. "Good-bye."

Whoop-whoop, blank screen.

What a world! What a new century! What am I doing in it? Okay, let's read the confounded script, get it over with.

Sorry, Aaron.

---

2. Yiddish, untranslatable. Literally, "turners." Roughly, "tricksters, rapscallions, wise guys."—HW

*Hollywood*THE *REPORTER*

UNKNOWN AS MOSES: REPORT

Nobody is talking at WarshaWorks, nor at Universal, where veteran Arnold Granit and fledgling writer-director Margolit Solovei have their offices. Reliable sources report, however, that an obscure Australian actor, Perry Michael Pines, is moving front and center to follow the late great Charlton Heston in the challenging role of Moses.

This development comes after protracted negotiations with several superstars broke down while preproduction costs have been mounting to DeMille scale. Financing of this tent-pole film, aimed at a worldwide audience of over two billion Christians and Muslims, has been the

(continued on page 14)

From: Perry Pines
To: Margolit Solovei
Subject: Rumors

Dear Ms. Solovei:

A little while ago I was out in the back paddock tagging lambs when my cell phone rang. It was my father. He's had three calls in an hour from *The Australian*, *The Adelaide Advertiser*, and *The Hobart Mercury*, about a story in *The Hollywood Reporter* that I've been cast as Moses. Of course he told them that he knew nothing about it. What is going on? Until I hear from you, be assured I'm not talking to anybody about this. Is it just more newspaper nonsense?

Perry Pines

Perry—it's Margo. An urgent policy meeting at WarshaWorks is scheduled for tomorrow morning. How wise of you to maintain silence about this fly-by-night *Reporter* story! Go on doing just that until you hear further from me tomorrow.

Chapter Nine

MARGO'S FLIGHT

(CONFERENCE RECORDED IN T. WARSHAW'S OFFICE. PRESIDING: MR. WARSHAW. ATTENDING: ARNOLD GRANIT, MARGO SOLOVEI.)

WARSHAW: Okay, let's begin, and to quote Eisenhower when the Battle of the Bulge broke out, *"This is not a disaster, it's an opportunity. There will be only smiling faces at this table . . ."*

SOLOVEI: Who isn't smiling?

GRANIT: Who indeed? My phones are ringing off the hook . . . e-mails and blogs snowing me under—it's a media lightning strike, no question—

WARSHAW: Me, I'm still stunned and shook up. To think that an unconfirmed leak could get the media buzzing around like smoked-out bees! Whatever happened to *"nobody cares about Moses anymore"*?

SOLOVEI: Yes, or *"One last rinse of DeMille's faded laundry,"* did you see that big snarky blog in the *Huffington Post*?

GRANIT: Where's Jacobs? Didn't you ask him to be here?

WARSHAW: He'll be along. He's at the Regency with a raging toothache, calling dentists all over town—

SOLOVEI: Why? I'll phone my dentist, he'll do anything for me—

WARSHAW: Let Hezzie take care of himself. We have a tiger by the tail here, troops, a PR explosion we didn't plan on and don't want, not yet . . . Margo, exactly what was in the Pines e-mail?

SOLOVEI: Got it right here. It's short and sensible.

(She reads the e-mail.)

WARSHAW: Sounds levelheaded.

GRANIT: Can we count on the fellow?

SOLOVEI: Until I respond, you can, but it should be soon.

WARSHAW: Damned soon! This business is spinning out of control now. I've made no offer, he has no representation. It's unheard-of legal exposure, he's down there in Australia tagging his lambs, free as air, loose as a goose. Maybe I should fly there—

GRANIT: Not so fast, that could unsettle him, put him on his guard—

WARSHAW: You have a point, but meantime, Heather in public relations is all steamed up, wants to do a press conference in Sydney, maybe even at the sheep farm—

GRANIT: What, *before* we get to him? Down-right idiotic—

SOLOVEI: Bloody *Hollywood Reporter*, who told them, anyway?

SPEAKERPHONE: Mr. Warshaw, I must see you immediately—

WARSHAW: Come ahead, Andrea—

(Andrea enters the office, hands Warshaw a paper, leaves.)

WARSHAW: *(reading the paper)* Kee-rist.

GRANIT: What?

WARSHAW: A fax from Jim Bearing in London. You had all better hear this. *(Mumbles.)* Mr. Timothy Warshaw, etc., etc. *(Reads aloud.)*

Dear Tim:

This is to advise you that Geoffrey Smallweed appeared in my office this morning. He wants ten million dollars—up front—for his client, Perry Pines, based on a story printed in yesterday's *Hollywood Reporter.* You'll recall that I urged you back in May (see my letter of the sixteenth) to pay the four thousand dollars he was asking, to void the Pines contract. Not hearing from you, I presumed you were not interested, and the matter lapsed.

How shall I handle this? Is there any substance to the story?

Sincerely, etc.

GRANIT: Why, Smallweed's insane, didn't Hezzie Jacobs pay him off months ago?
WARSHAW: Of course! I asked Hezzie to pay the four thousand, and he did. *(On speakerphone)* Andrea?
ANDREA: *(on speakerphone)* Yes, sir?
WARSHAW: Get Mr. Jacobs at the Hyatt Regency, and bring me the transcript of our May sixteenth conference.
ANDREA: *(on speakerphone)* Very well.
GRANIT: On second thought, Tim, maybe you *should* fly there, even today—

(Andrea enters with papers.)

ANDREA: Mr. Jacobs's line is busy. Here's the transcript, sir.

(She leaves. Warshaw flips through the papers.)

WARSHAW: Okay, here we are.
(Reads.)

WARSHAW: Wait, Arnie, one bit of business. Jim Bearing reports that Smallweed is down to four thousand dollars, and he urges that I take it. Hezzie, can you advance that?

JACOBS: Me? Four thousand? Who's Smallweed? What's it all about?

WARSHAW: Look, Hezzie, Andrea will fill you in on Smallweed. I don't want the item on our cost report. You know Gluck—

JACOBS: Well, I guess I can handle four thousand.

WARSHAW: What could be plainer?

ANDREA: *(on speakerphone)* Mr. Jacobs, on three—

WARSHAW: Hezzie, how are you?

JACOBS: *(on speakerphone, groaning)* I'm in horrible shape, why?

WARSHAW: Sorry to hear it. Listen, you took care of that Smallweed thing, didn't you?

JACOBS: *(very hoarse and low)* Smallweed? Oh, the four-thousand-dollars business? Of course— Look, Tim, what's with these Hollywood dentists? You try to talk to them, a snotty girl says you can see the doctor in four weeks—

SOLOVEI: *(calls out)* Hezzie, Margo here. I've got a message in to my doc to see you today, I'll check—

GRANIT: *(calling out)* Hezzie, Arnie here. Bearing says he never got your four thousand, and Smallweed's asking for ten million dollars —

JACOBS: *What?* Bearing's a liar, and Smallweed is a fucking lunatic—pardon my French, Margo. Can you really get me in, save my life?

WARSHAW: Hezzie, *please* check with your office, confirm that you paid the money—

JACOBS: Will do. What time is it in Houston? I'm in a fog of pain.

SOLOVEI: *(calls out)* Okay, Hezzie, Dr. Kline will take you. I'll pick you up at the Regency—

JACOBS: *(groans)* I'll be waiting outside. You're an angel of mercy, toots. Marry me!

(Conference adjourns until 2:00 p.m.)

Hello, Perry! It's Margo. I just want you to know I read out your e-mail at the conference, and Mr. Warshaw had high praise for your "level head." We're on a break now. So far, so good. More later today.

Dearest Mashie:

Bless you, thank you! Fridja can't stop raving about our Hollywood adventure, the way you found time, busy as you are, to run us round Universal, give us lunch in your Catalina cottage, and even take her for a barefoot walk on the beach! She says you're not just a sister-in-law, you're a true lovely sister. I'll write again from Hong Kong, about the wedding. It was awesome, and one of these days I may just move my base to São Paulo. Brazil is where it's at these days, Brazil and China. I'm the happiest man alive.

Beshie

SOLOVEI: *(entering)* Confirmed: Hezzie's office did send Bearing the money. Poor Hezzie's back at the Regency—he's shot full of dope and off in la-la land. Seems he needs a root canal—

WARSHAW: Bummer—

ANDREA: *(entering and distributing papers)* Letter of intent. *(Exits.)*

GRANIT: *(scanning)* One page. Fine, the simpler, the better.

WARSHAW: *(nodding)* This does it, and the only person to bring it to Pines is you, Margo, hand to hand.

GRANIT: Wait, you're the boss, Tim. A terrific gesture if you fly to see him yourself—

SOLOVEI: Right!

WARSHAW: Wrong, he trusts only you. You've been his advocate. Once he knows you're flying there we're all right, though we can't stay ahead of this for long. I'm talking days—

GRANIT: The damnedest thing. The role of a century offered to a bit player, and nothing but problems.

SOLOVEI: Well, but this is a jolt, gents, I've been racing on the script to finish up—

WARSHAW: Work on the plane. Sixteen hours or more, with nothing to do. First off, phone him that you're coming.

SOLOVEI: Absolutely not! He'd be as staggered as I am—

WARSHAW: He'll be enchanted. You're his goddess. Do it.

GRANIT: *(into speakerphone)* Andrea, get me Slim Wheatley at the Van Nuys Airport—

ANDREA: *(on speakerphone)* Yes, Mr. Granit—

SOLOVEI: Well, I'm all in a whirl. What would the weather be like now down there? How do I dress for a sheep farm?

WARSHAW: Do you have your passport handy?

SOLOVEI: Yes, but the whole airport mess—the crowds, the security lines, the pat-downs—

WARSHAW: Forget it, you're going by company jet—

ANDREA: *(on speakerphone)* Mr. Granit, Slim isn't there. Here's his copilot, Bill Falk.

GRANIT: Hi, Bill? You and Slim are taking Margolit Solovei to Australia. Confidential meeting, zero profile.

FALK: *(on speakerphone)* Understood, Mr. Granit. Just one passenger?

GRANIT: Just one. Tell Slim to call me.

FALK: *(on speakerphone)* Yes, sir. I'll let Slim know and start fueling up.

WARSHAW: This conference is over.

SOLOVEI: The lousy hell it is! I want a day, I mean a day starting now, to pull myself together—

WARSHAW: You've got it. Go!

From: Margolit Solovei
To: Deborah Kamaiko
Subject: Wedding Announcement

Aloft, Burbank to Sydney

Mazel tov to you and Cy! Great news! Your e-mail came as I was throwing things into a suitcase. Now I'm in a WarshaWorks jet, a big posh Falcon, whizzing me to Australia as I draft the last scenes of my screenplay, cosseted by two hunky pilots. In rifts in the clouds far below I see the wrinkling blue Pacific, nothing else. It's a hush-hush trip, Debbie. Mum's the word.

Now about the wedding, Josh is perfect for Cy's best man, of course, and I'm deeply moved that you want me for your maid of honor. But my very dear, don't we have a different relationship? We've never met face-to-face! If I'm filming by then, an overnight round-trip would do it, that's no problem. I just fear that the rare magic of our candid "Shaw-Terry" correspondence might evaporate. Maybe this is a stupid reaction, batted off while writing the death of Moses. I'm up in the air in more ways than one, Debbie, indeed in my whole life. More about that another time. Meantime back to Mt. Nebo.

Ever your
Margo

P.S. By the bye, any news of the Hviesten/ Scharf runaways? I'm shamefully interested in that reality sitcom. M.

From: Deborah Kamaiko
To: Margo Solovei
Subject: The Veneerings

Bless my soul, Baroness von Munchausen, I can't keep up with you. Private jet to Australia, "hunky pilots," what next? About the maid of honor, dear, you may well be right. There's time to decide, lots of time.

Now, about the runaways, I have juicy news indeed. Remember the phony Veneerings in *Our Mutual Friend*? That's our runaways to the life. Avram told Hviesten he was a big real estate operator, and Hviesten told Avram her parents owned lots of downtown Trondheim real estate. Turns out her father owns a small lumberyard out of town, and of course our Arthur/Avram is stony-broke. Cy phoned Shirley, curious about Hviesten, and she told him all this with ghoulish glee. She says he's tweeting her like mad for the price of a ticket home. She's just letting him crawl, and meantime he's eating humble pie at the table of the lumberman. The table talk should be interesting.

Enough! Like you, I feel guilty, enjoying this "reality sitcom"—felicitous phrase! Back to work, both of us. Best of luck with your final pages of Moses, and happy landings on your hush-hush mission.

Ever with love,

Debbie

From: Perry Pines
To: Margolit Solovei
Subject: Robertson Farm

Dear Ms. Solovei:

Lem Robertson, our well-off neighbor, has a private jet, and he tells Pa that the landing strip on his sheep farm can accommodate a Falcon, though his plane is smaller. Lem's pilot is Carey Glenn. Your pilot should contact Carey before you land in Sydney Airport. Clearing customs in Sydney, especially for private aircraft, is not simple. (I hope you don't have a favorite cat or dog along!) Carey will fill him in on flying to Lem's place. Of course I can't wait to see you again and learn the news you bring! Such suspense would go good in a movie.

Meantime, all my best.

Perry

Carey Glenn's stats:
            Phone: (03) 9714-6730
            E-mail: CareyG@flyby.com

From: Margolit Solovei
To: Herman Wouk
Subject: *Tam v'nishlam*[1]

Dear Mr. Wouk:

My screenplay is finished! You, of all people, know what that means—reading the whole thing over from Page 1 to face what's actually there on paper. For you, maybe a thousand pages of lasting prose. For me, a meager 107 pages of a mere blueprint for the movie Arnold Granit and I still have to make.

You were right—or maybe it was your formidable wife—compelling me to finish the script before you would evaluate it. I hope it will endure your scrutiny.

WarshaWorks is flying me all by myself to Australia in a company jet to bring Perry Pines a contract offer. I daresay you're aware of the media fuss over the story in the *Hollywood Reporter*. It

---

1. Closing words to a rabbinic work: "finished and complete."
—HW

happens to be true. Not a word of this, of course, until Tim Warshaw announces it. I write you from 35,000 feet above the empty, empty Pacific, *Caine Mutiny* waters! I wrote a book report about your novel in Bais Yaakov and got an A. I really ate up that one "racy" scene in Yosemite. Our teacher said you must have stuck that in to sell books.

Just me unwinding . . .

With gratitude and profound respect,

Margo

From: Herman Wouk
To: Margolit Solovei
Subject: Your Script

Tam v'nishlam, eh? Your roots go deep, and from them you've drawn (know it or not) the fortitude and the energy charge to take on and finish your *Moses*. When can I expect to see the script? Your mission to Pines sounds like a steep Warshaw gamble. Still, old Gluck did say at the screen test, *"But that's Moishe Rabenu,"* and Warshaw's betting the farm on that. Good luck to him and you.

About my Yosemite scene: Bais Yaakov girls are mighty sheltered and inhibited creatures. I well remember! In my dim, distant past I went out with one or two. I'm surprised your rebbetzin even let you write a report on *Mutiny*. The principal of one such school vainly proposed that he prepare a bowdlerized *Mutiny* edition cutting out the "love stuff" (i.e., Yosemite), as we Bronx kids called the mushy moments in cowboy movies.

I'll await your screenplay with interest. It'll be a brief respite from my dogged travail on my own

218

version of *Moses*. At least you've finished yours. I'm racing the calendar, and don't seem to be gaining.

With high regard and best wishes,

HW

From: Arnold Granit
To: Margolit Solovei
Subject: Smallweed Bombshell

Margo,

I trust you're enjoying your Falcon ride, but I must interrupt to let you know that Bearing has received Hezzie's $4,000, five months too late! There was a foul-up in the electronic transfer of bank funds. Bearing admits his office was entirely at fault. Smallweed of course becomes a serious problem, though Tim is astonishingly cool about it. Extreme stress is his Jacuzzi, it relaxes him. Now he wants you to get, by any and all means, a copy of Smallweed's contract with Perry Pines.

Affectionate best,

Arnie

From: Mashie
To: Josh
Subject: HELP!

Josh, my very dear,

The damsel is in distress again, this time in a private jet approaching Fiji! We're refueling before going on to Australia. I'm sure you know about that *Hollywood Reporter* leak and the ensuing hoo-ha. The brunt of it all is now on my shoulders, to wit:

[Margo summarizes the electronic mishap in Bearing's office, Pines's rabid hatred of his ex-agent, her mission to sign him up for the part, and now Warshaw's demand that she obtain a copy of the Smallweed contract.]

Dear, I don't know quite how I handle this. Perry Pines is devoted to me. He trusts me. I presume he's heard from Smallweed, and if I ask him for the contract, won't that alert him to Warshaw's problem with that "bottom-feeder"? How can I truthfully respond if he asks questions? I dread facing Perry and his father in the Sydney airport. This is a shout for quick advice. In any case, I'll bull through as I can and let you know how it's going.

Isn't it great about Debbie and Cy getting married? She wants me for maid of honor. I love her, we've become remarkably intimate pen pals, and maybe I'll do it. If so, there you and I will be, standing together under a chuppah, as though I need more confusion in my life.

Not so incidentally, I finished my screenplay. Finished it in flight, actually. A long plane trip is great for working. I don't dare look back at it now. I'm killing time reading a dull aviation magazine until we land.

Yours,

Mashie

From: Josh
To: Mashie
Subject: Help

Sweetie, you're confused, all right. If I were back in D.C. I'd now be dead asleep, twelve time zones away. As it happens, I'm at Nullarbor Ponds, Hezzie Jacobs's huge algae project in southwest Australia. More about that another time, but straight to your quandary. An offer for the role of Moses! Naturally the actor will greet you with joy, and of course he'll sign the letter of intent. As for the contract, Smallweed's lawyer was probably a bottom-feeder like himself, and the contract—if he's kept a copy—will be a sieve. Just tell Pines that Warshaw wants it, that's the plain truth. You're a tough cookie (I'm an authority on that), so keep your cool and breeze through these next hours, alert and lighthearted. All will go well.

And so you've finished your screenplay—determined, dared, and done! You're one of a kind, blast you.

Love,

Josh

From: Marvin Zivoni
To: Weizmann Institute
Subject: Nullarbor settlement

We have a royalty agreement. Adin Genakowski proposed the deal, Joshua Lewin agreed, so Dr. Gillespie caved. Mr. Jacobs approved by Skype. There will be no income for five years, if ever, it's all been a dispute over highly speculative eventual royalties. Genakowski's prestige tipped the balance. The Nobel rumors about him abound among us geneticists.

I am bringing home the papers for the Institute's signature.

Marvin

From: Margolit Solovei
To: Tim Warshaw
CC: Arnold Granit
Subject: Perry Pines

Tim:

You and Arnold should be pleased. Moishe Rabenu has signed your Letter of Agreement, and I have his Smallweed contract. I'm jet-lagged and wrung out. Perry's parents have kindly put me up in a nice guest bedroom for the night. More tomorrow.

Margo

From: Mashie
To: Josh
Subject: Updates

Sorry about the time zone idiocy. Believe me, I am utterly disoriented, and not just on time zones. The encounter at the Sydney airport couldn't have been easier or pleasanter! Sometimes I think you're clairvoyant. Everything went as you predicted, smooth as oil. Perry and his dad flew back with me in the Falcon to a landing strip near their ranch. He did hear from Smallweed, but simply deleted the e-mail as addled nonsense. We talked all the way, and we'd settled our business by the time we landed. His dad even got in some heartwarming pleasantries about my *Zuleika* movie. The landing was some-thing, swooping down over thou-sands and thousands of frightened sheep scampering about! I'm sitting up in bed in the farm-house, and I've just e-mailed Tim that I've got the signed letter and the Smallweed contract. I snuggled down and turned out the light, thinking I'd drop off as I hit the pillow, but no, my head is spinning with jet-lagged thoughts. Hence this brief update. Now, what on *earth* are you up to at Hezzie's algae ponds?

Thanks, dear, for your encouraging words when I needed them. I did "breeze" through the business talk on the plane, churning inside but Jane Austen outside. You know me. You should.

Ever your

Hollywood Jane

From: Josh
To: Mashie
Subject: Update

Well done, Jane A.! Now I can level with you. Believe me, you were in a damned nasty spot. Warshaw had his colossal nerve gambling on you that way, but it's how he survives. I just tried to psych you up, like the coach of a nervous finalist. You'd have pulled it off anyway, I'm sure. If I helped a bit, good.

You ask what I'm doing here. It's a story. The hostelry I'm in now, called Uluru Tents, is at the dead center of the outback. Flat empty desert horizon to horizon, all sand and scrub, out of which heaves one marvelous apparition, a vast red monolith that the British dubbed Ayers Rock. The aborigines, who hold it in religious awe, know it as Uluru. I'm with the aborigines. It's out there in the morning light as I write, and I'm awed and God-haunted, almost as at shofar blasts on Rosh Hashanah. I'd never heard of Uluru, and I wouldn't be here, let alone in Australia, if not for Adin Genakowski, a guy almost as strange as that Rock. He dragged me here, and he's out there climbing Uluru right now.

[Josh sums up the algae dispute and the geneticist's intervention, after the Hecht Lecture, to bring Zivoni and Gillespie together . . .]

. . . Gillespie and Zivoni went at it for two days in their opaque jargon of molecular biology. Adin's comments were like sun breaking through fog. A Feynman of genetics pretty near, or so he strikes me. About the settlement, he summed up, "Ghost royalties, gentlemen, on ghost gasoline in about 2025. Maybe! Shake hands." They did.

Among his oddities, Adin is a rabid travel freak. On his sabbaticals he forgets genetics and goes to places like Nepal and Machu Picchu. He took on the Hecht Lecture partly because he could then get to Nullarbor, bring the profs together, do some whale watching, and then go on to Ayers Rock. Today he flies off east to scuba dive the Great Barrier Reef. He tried to drag me with him—says he can't scuba dive either, there are guides that train you and take you far down in the coral. Ha! Me, I'm doing exactly nothing all day after a week's bellyful of paperwork, just watch the sun setting on the Rock and get a decent night's sleep. In the morning I fly Qantas from Alice Springs to Washington, DC.

Love,

Josh

From: Tim Warshaw
To: Margolit Solovei

Margo! You came through like the United States Marines! The campaign for Perry Pines is already in the works. Just fax copies of that Smallweed contract to me and Jim Bearing pronto. *Vanity Fair* wants to interview Perry Pines, would you believe it? Give Moishe Rabenu my best, and tell him to brace himself for a grand ride. Take an extra day or two off on the way home. Fiji's beautiful, and the Falcon is yours till Monday.

Tim

From: Arnold Granit
To: Margolit Solovei

You witch, I knew you would pull it off. The glad shock was the final Mount Nebo scene that you faxed me from the plane. It will work beautifully, and it's all straight Scripture. You've been getting better as you go. These last pages are torn from the heart of one possessed. All the wheels are turning now. We'll make this movie in a year, and it will be terrific. I'm proud of my protégée. Congrats and love, hurry back.

Arnie

From: Mashie
To: Josh

Dearest Josh—

God, do I feel marvelous! A long deep sleep in a soft farmhouse bed, breathing clear sweet Southern Hemisphere air, then very early this morning a long walk with Perry among his leaping lambs, watching him tag their ears amid great discordant bleating everywhere. He's a most unactorish actor, shy, sweet, yet quietly formidable. I'm back at the farmhouse, going through my e-mails. The huzzahs from Hollywood have me a bit drunk with power. Warshaw has released the Falcon to me for a holiday in Fiji! Last night I saw the Southern Cross, somewhat askew but the real thing, a jeweled spectacle as glorious as our Orion up north. I just Googled this Uluru Tents you're in. After your rhapsodic rave—shofar blasts on Rosh Hashanah, indeed!—Fiji can wait, my first stop is Ayers Rock. When will I have another chance to see this aboriginal Mount Sinai?—or for that matter, you again, on the upside-down side of the world? My pilot Slim knows the Tents well, he's reserved two rooms in the main house, one for me, one for himself and his copilot. I hope this Adin Genakowski hasn't left before I get there. He sounds almost as intriguing as Ayers Rock. Is he married?

Always your fond unattached,

Mashie

From: Josh
To: Mashie

Booming guns! Soaring rockets! Sousa brass band fortissimo!! Last night I choked off the suggestion that you come here, wrote you four e-mails and one by one deleted them, no words seemed right. Now you've decided it yourself, great! As for the main house, forget it, you can't see anything from there. Since you're suddenly such a brazen wench drunk with power, I tell you that a tent is the only place, and a few are vacant, but you'll stay overnight here with me, and none of this *It Happened One Night* stuff, Janie, forget it. These "tents" are really luxurious little lodges with canvas roofs facing the Rock across empty desert, accommodating one to four people, with a thick sliding divider. Adin slept last night on the other side of it, and a good thing, too. He's a wonderful guy, possibly a genius, but he snores like a garbage truck climbing uphill. I found that out at Nullarbor, and had to demand another room. He wasn't offended, it's an old story to him. Now then, when you arrive have your stuff brought to Tent 5 with your winsome self. Adin may still be here. When I told him you were coming he tried to postpone his charter flight to Cairns, and he's still trying.

Love,

Josh

(E-MAIL)

From: Mashie
To: Josh

Done. We'll be arriving midafternoon. Urge Adin to hang in there.

The Wench

From: Joshua Lewin
To: Timothy Warshaw

Dear Mr. Warshaw:

I'm in Australia on an arbitration case, and have met Margo at a hotel near Ayers Rock, Australia's big natural wonder. She's flying on to Fiji in the morning, and asked me to write you. I gather she did well in her mission. She obtained and showed me the Smallweed contract that so concerned you. It's badly wrinkled and blurred by rain, as Pines had stowed it in a leaky shed with a lot of other old papers. I've managed to read it and make notes. The thing is poorly done, here and there actually ungram-matical—nothing to worry about in my view. I'm bringing it to you on my Qantas flight to DC tomorrow, at Margo's request.

Joshua Lewin

From: Margolit Solovei
To: Deborah Kamaiko

Dearest Debbie:

This has to go fast. Guess what? I'm stark naked, under a hotel bathrobe, about to shower in a luxurious "tent," or canvas-roofed bungalow, where I'll be spending the night with Josh Lewin. Wait, wait, don't be scandalized or excited, this isn't your hotel room thing with Cy, not on your life. This place is completely partitioned by a thick canvas divider. He's on the other side working on an e-mail to my producer. The hush-hush mission has been a rip-roaring success, and tomorrow I fly to Fiji for a day or two. Try Googling "Uluru Tents," and you'll get some hotel boiler-plate with pictures of the bungalow, and the marvel of nature called Uluru. Josh's in Australia on legal business, I found out and suggested this Ayers Rock for a rendezvous. He jumped at it, calling me a "brazen wench," a quaint locution which made me feel warm all over. Now for my first shower in three or four days. Not sure which, I'm all jet-lagged and in a tizzy. More news after the break, don't go away!

All love,

Margo

From: Adin Genakowski
To: Margolit Solovei
Subject: Those fifteen minutes

Dear Margolit Solovei:

Our chat while Josh looked through that blurry contract was a revelation. I've been curious about you because of his years of unrequited devotion. Now I understand him.

Strange! You've thrown off a Hasidic upbringing, yet it has to be in your blood and bones. I'm a pathetic outsider, all black hat, spiky black whiskers and no depth. Josh is the golden mean. Great fellow. He forgave me my snoring, which any woman will have to do before I can get serious with her. Josh deserves you, it is written in both your genes. There as you know I speak with authority. In fact, with equal authority I've found a tie in my genes to those of an Israeli girl, Hepzibah Zivoni. Now I have to convince her, since she brushed me off as a "secular Jew in masquerade." Since she is so discerning and dismissive, she will be mine. I thrive on challenge.

To you and Josh, all blessings from a fraud in transit,

Adin Genakowski

Chapter Ten

MARGO'S MOSES II

(E-MAIL)

From: Margolit Solovei
To: Deborah Kamaiko
Subject: Update

Dearest Debbie:

What is your opinion of Robert Louis
Stevenson? One doesn't hear about him
much these days.

And if you ask me what the devil Stevenson
has to do with anything, at the moment
I'm in Samoa, where he's buried, reeling a
bit from drinking kava with my pilots in
the hotel bar, and weary and footsore
from visiting his grave. Fiji was overrun
with tourists, and anyway once we got
there all I wanted to do was sleep, as you
can guess. Riffling a travel guide over
coffee next morning, I noted that Samoa
was an air trip an hour and a half away.

By God, I thought, that's more like it, I don't expect to command a private jet again in my lifetime, we go to Samoa! The pilot, Slim, said, "Samoa? No problem." Lovely feeling!

You see, Debbie, in the Bais Yaakov library when I was ten or so, I came on a faded set of Stevenson that somebody had donated. I raced through those dusty books like a forest fire, from the birdie with the yellow bill to *Weir of Hermiston*, and I will always love Stevenson, though I've seldom looked at his work since. I visited his mountain home (now a museum) and then climbed a long narrow dirt path through dense greenery to his grave at the very peak, a squarish concrete tomb with metal plaques hard to read, all black-streaked with mold. *Sic transit*!

I'm off to eat Polynesian food with the pilots. Tomorrow, nonstop plunge back into reality via the Burbank airport, where I turn in my magic carpet.

Love,

Margo

JAMES C. BEARING
BARRISTER
77 BOND STREET
LONDON, W1, ENGLAND

Dear Tim:

Re: Smallweed

Thanks for the photocopy of that rain-blurred contract. Kudos to Margo Solovei! I concur with you and Lewin that the document is amateurishly drawn up. Smallweed may well have done it himself. From a legal standpoint, it's a null. Today he telephoned me, reducing his price to nine million, providing I close within the next twenty-four hours. Absolutely final offer, otherwise it's ten million and he goes straight to the media. I've invited him to my office to "negotiate." He's coming at ten tomorrow, and I rather look forward to it.

Best regards,

Jim

From: Deborah Kamaiko
To: Margolit Solovei
Subject: Stevenson??? Magic Carpet??

Why, you devious creature, how *dare* you leave me hanging, checking my e-mail by the hour, having trouble sleeping! *"More to come after the break. Stay tuned."* And you stark naked in a tent with Josh Lewin! Honestly, Margo, you're too much. Humble schoolmarm though I am, I don't have to put up with such nonsense from my queenly Hollywood pen pal. *What happened next?* Come on!

As for Stevenson—and isn't that like you, casting a fly to a scholarly trout whose field is Victorian lit—your encounter with him was a lucky early awakening to English prose and masterly story-telling. Stevenson has a "submerged" reputation, goes on being read all over the world. Besides his stroke of genius, Jekyll and Hyde, he did write much that lasts. Like the far greater Twain, he peaked in a couple of boys' books, in fact, the comparison would do for a dissertation. It will damn well do for my snap at the fly, you miserable tease!

Love,

Debbie

From: Perry Pines
To: Margolit Solovei
Subject: Quandary

Dear Ms. Solovei:

You've been my guardian angel in this whole Moses business, which still seems like a waking dream. A reporter with a TV truck is parked outside the main gate to our farm. My dad and mum take turns answering phone calls from the media and saying nothing. About the letter of intent, big Hollywood agencies have sure been after me, but I'm a burnt child. No agent! My old dad has come up with an idea. All he knows is sheep farming—not that I know much more—but he's pretty down to earth, not like me. Lem Robertson's two sons, Bill and Marty, have wives who both want to live in Melbourne or maybe Sydney. Lem is a diabetic, he's slowed way down. There's been talk that he wants to sell Robertson Station, which partly borders on our west paddock. Pa has a good notion of Lem's asking price, and that, Pa says, should be my price to do

244

Moses. We'd need a good stateside lawyer to handle it, but because the moneyman, Mr. Gluck, approved of me to play the part, I'm in the catbird seat, as Pa puts it. Please, will you write me what you think about all this? I trust you.

Sincerely,

Perry

From: Margolit Solovei
To: Deborah Kamaiko
Subject: CENSORED!

Spare me your mock indignation, sweetie. If I know you—and I think I do, sight unseen—when you read my first words about Stevenson, you burst out laughing. Anticlimax is a tool of Wilde's wit, *n'est-ce pas*? I just wasn't up to writing "what happened next" so soon.

When Josh sent me that e-mail rave about Ayers Rock I couldn't know what he had in mind, but I could guess. I let him know I was on my way. He responded with "Booming guns, soaring rockets, Sousa brass band fortissimo," plus, he assured me that the only way to view the Red Rock was from the tents, not from the main house, I had to stay with him in his tent, but no problem, there was this canvas divider and so forth. Subtle as a charging bull, I thought. I'd made the first move but there were the proprieties, and before we got there I told Slim to book dinner for four at the main house. Josh had no choice.

Next, into that famous shower, and on to dinner. The pilots and I had roast lamb and good red Australian wine. He orders a Caesar salad for his main course, telling the waiter, "No bacon bits," exactly as in the old days. A bit sobering, that. Ah, but the rascal is still so handsome, receding hairline or no, still so subtly beguiling! The pilots liked him. He told them about Cy, turned out Slim knew a fellow in Cy's unit, and they talked war and politics while I devoured lamb, feeling somewhat uncomfortable (after all this time!) because he was downing only lettuce without bacon bits. I dawdled long over the dessert. My giddy mood before the shower had quite subsided. Now that the moment was upon me, I was in no hurry at all to walk back with him through the night to that tent.

Yet once there, he embraced and kissed me, most natural thing in the world, and for a while it was just sweet and familiar. We went out and sat on the patio. Full moon on Uluru, a monstrous silvered shape rearing up against the stars. I talked about Perry Pines, he told me more about the algae business. The old animal attraction hung around us in the dusk like a heavy perfume. The long years seemed to dissolve. He mentioned again his flight to Washington early next morning. "Off at the crack of dawn! If I'd only known! But this is fine, thank God for this, it's miraculous—"

"It's also ridiculous," I blurted. "Why can't we see a little more of each other, after all? Four hours by air, whenever we like? Just friends?"

"I'm available," he said. We looked at each other and both broke into relieved guffaws, at everything we *weren't* saying. It was his moment to pull me to my feet and make his move if ever, wasn't it? Well, he didn't do it. Why? Thinking of his early flight? He just stood up with a tired sigh, "Bedtime, alas." Guys can be exasperating, Debbie, can't they just! You never know. The tent had little bathrooms on each side of the divider. We wished each other good night, he slides the divider shut, and that was it.

Talk about anticlimax! But of course he was only being sensible. Columbia Law School sensible! No point, after all the estranged years, for the two of us to flop into a one-night stand in the Australian outback! Only sensible . . . yet there I lay in a soft, wide bed for two, totally wide awake, memories revolving in disorder, way back to meeting him at the engagement party, forward to that one kiss when he made the red-eye round-trip . . . the arguments, the sexy wrestlings, the breakups and reconciliations . . . and more futile wrestlings long after we'd formally broken up . . . thoughts of other guys too, who came and went, I'm all too human, Debbie, but they all were nothing, nothing compared to Josh, flares that fizzled . . .

(Whoops, crazy turbulence. Slim just staggered back here, said it would last maybe half an hour, can't type. . . . Later: it lasted an hour, smooth as oil now, hope I haven't lost the thread, quite a shaking up! Deep breath . . .)

After about an hour or so of this I got up, unfastened the divider, slipped through, and got into his bed. He was dead asleep. He grunted, "Huh? What?" I said, "Nothing, just the brazen wench. I'm cold." With that he turns over and stares. "You? You? Do you know what you're doing?" I didn't think, it just came out, "Hell, yes." With that, wow, he crushes the breath out of me. "Great! Glory be, you're mine," and he mutters something in Hebrew.

The bursting of a dam, Debbie, the dammed-up love of years cascading through a few wild hours, lovemaking, laughing, endearments, more lovemaking —an orgy, I tell you, we didn't sleep at all, we ended in worn-out bliss slinging Shakespeare quotes at each other (I swear!) as Uluru reddened in the dawn.

Must you be gone? says I as he leaves the bed. *It was the nightingale, and not the lark . . .*

He's back at me, thumb pointing at the Rock,

I must be gone,
Night's candles are burnt out, and jocund day
Stands tiptoe on the misty mountaintops . . .

He's gone, and there I am lying amid the bedclothes, searching my deliciously numbed mind for a Shakespeare comeback. I stumble back to "my" side, still in my birth-day suit, start putting myself to rights; and am brushing my hair when I hear the divider sliding. There he is ready to go, by God, zipping up his wheeled airline suitcase. By now it's broad day. I'm poised with another quote, *Pray, tarry!* *You men will never tarry . . .*

"No, no, love, withdraw that!" He laughs. "That's Cressida, Shakespeare loathed her, in those few words she skewers herself as an easy lay—"

"Right, withdrawn! I'll settle for your 'brazen wench.' Oh, Josh, you ruffian, you're off and here I am, and look at those sheets, will you?"

"Mashie, darling, Lord love you, no problem, Uluru Tents is a honeymoon hotel. Cost of doing business."

The lawyerish phrase strikes my funny bone, his too, and we're laughing, laughing and kissing, a lot of that, and whiz he's gone. In all that rapturous time to the very last, nothing was said about "what comes next," dear friend, nothing at all. Best I can do. Read and burn.

Margo

P.S. Since then we've been texting plenty about what comes next as we fly in opposite directions around the globe. Again, read and burn! M.

From: Margolit Solovei
To: Perry Pines

Perry—I'll be landing in a couple of hours. The pilot just told me that Tim Warshaw and the others will be at the airport to hail the conquering heroine. Remember, I'm on "the other side," so I can't give you advice on terms. If you want a stateside lawyer, I can recommend a bang-up one. I'll never forget the lambs. Best to your parents, M.

Moses Film Memo No. 19

Well, I've been through Margo's screenplay twice. I may have done a very dumb thing. After I finished I took Candy for a turn around the garden, then I pulled out my filed chapters of *Aaron's Diary* and read them over. Oddly, the two scripts are almost the same length, but what a difference! By page 103 she has told the whole story, whereas on my page 107, Aaron is being hounded by the mob to give them a god, i.e., the Golden Calf, while Moses is away up on Sinai. This is not a cheering comparison.

BSW is in the living room, steno pad on her lap, reading the screenplay with slow concentration, her business mode. When she stopped for lunch, not a word about the screenplay. It's close to dinnertime now, and she's about two-thirds through the pages. My guess is I'll hear nothing until tomorrow. Meantime, the WarshaWorks people are twisting in the wind. The decision's up to me, which means up to BSW, who'll have the last word as usual. Me, I'm in a deep, deep down.

Margo has done her job. Not too much to say about that. She sent me the first half of the script from the Ahwahnee Hotel, and this is just the rest of it. I don't think she could have done much better. Her knowledge of the Torah, drilled into her by her Hasidic father, gives this frail Hollywood artifact a tang of truth, and her residual love of him some warmth. He is Margo's Moses, and the thing might just work as the ground of a retro DeMille blockbuster. Given the money, that's what Hollywood does: turn meager words into glorious pictures that move, mostly ephemera, but all depends on the story. Solovei has the storytelling instinct. This story recorded millennia ago on rolled-up animal skins—such as us Jews still unroll once a week to read from on Shabbat—holds yet in varying versions for half the planet's believers. Of course she wasn't up to telling it right. Who is?

Who indeed? And so I come to *Aaron's Diary.* With the usual ups and downs, the exaltations and despairs, of writing a novel, the book attempts a truly new word picture of the Lawgiver, half-seen through a veil of awed respect by Aaron, who's been dragged into greatness late in life by his kid brother, Moses, the pampered lad who disappeared from Pharaoh's palace half a lifetime ago on the run, now a God-driven bearded giant. Aaron is doing his best to serve as his brother's mouthpiece, recording it all with somewhat bewildered wry irony. It hasn't been easy for me to keep up the vein. How for instance can ironic humor handle the sudden death of his two sons when fire from heaven strikes the altar?

I have absolutely no idea. I plod toward that challenge as I once did toward the scary Battle of Midway, day by day, page by page. Challenges yield to persistence; or until now they have.

What happened to me in the garden this afternoon was a stab of perception about *Aaron's Diary*. As Margo has doggedly used her story-telling craft to grind out her Lawgiver, haven't I doggedly fallen back on my sense of humor to do my Moses? Writing jokes for radio comedians was the way I first made my living. Isn't *Aaron's Diary*, after all, just a gagman's Moses?

My enigmatic BSW likes it so far. Up to a point, that's reassuring. I call to mind one rainy after-noon some sixty years ago, when I paced amid dripping trees in Kings Point, despairing of the *Mutiny* as just a litany of petty gripes about a lousy captain I had at sea, just one more postwar "revenge book," trivial and best-sellerish. In my thirties, that was a dismal low point, and she cheered me out of it. In my latter nineties—well—let's hear what BSW has to say about Margo's Moses, anyway. Meanwhile let's do another page or two of Aaron's confounded diary.

James C. Bearing
Barrister
77 Bond Street
London W1, England

Mr. Timothy Warshaw
WarshaWorks
Century City, California 90067

Dear Tim:

Re: Smallweed

Attached is a witnessed copy of Geoffrey Small-weed's release of Perry Pines. He arrived early, and Orly handed him a photocopy of the rain-blurred contract, with a smooth copy which I had red-inked paragraph by paragraph. After a while he came into my office with those papers in hand. The release was on my desk beside a stack of British pounds. This was, you will recall, the original settlement he'd accepted, then tried to renege on it. He kept glancing at the currency as we talked. (To quote the poet Byron, "Ready money is Aladdin's lamp.") Our conversation was not long, it soon became clear that my red-ink notes had quite disarmed him. He signed the release, pocketed the £5,000, and departed. The settlement payment advanced by our office will be billed to you in due course.

Faithfully,

James Bearing

Enclosure

BETTY SARAH WOUK

Hi, I hear you typing away, I hope on <u>Aaron's Diary</u>, so I won't interrupt you. Here are my stenopad notes on Solovei's scenario. They don't amount to much, no point discussing them. I can't judge a screenplay. If I'd been asked for an opinion on the DeMille screenplay for <u>The Ten Commandments</u>, I'd have voted against it, for idiotic inaccuracy and a bogus main character Nefretiri, or whatever. It's considered one of the greatest films of all time, so there you are. When you're through working I do have one question we should discuss.

<u>Moses Film Memo No. 20</u>

I went to get coffee, found the above note in my box, and called her into the office. "What's the question?"

"Let's talk about it tonight."

"No, we talk about it now."

"Very well." She takes the Eames chair. Between us on the desk, framed, is the small picture she sent me in a love letter that came by sea mail off Okinawa. Silence, then she comes out with it. "Are you capable of saying no?"

Just the kind of question that girl in the picture would spring on me. Hence seven decades later she sits in that armchair. (One of the reasons.) I take my time before responding. "It's not that bad, surely?"

"And if it is? With everything that's at stake— aborting a project that's already cost millions— giving Solovei a black eye she'll never live down—possibly throwing WarshaWorks into bankruptcy without Gluck's 'stimulus'—with all that, you're really capable of saying no?"

Pinned to the wall, not the first time in nigh seventy years. "Well, your opinion matters a lot—"

She wrinkles her mouth, with a slight headshake. "Okay, okay. You've painted yourself into a corner and you know it. You've done no work on this film, just wasted a lot of time. Solovei tried to consult you on the Golden Calf scene, but luckily you ducked it—"

"Your doing—"

"Yes, that time you listened. Your name on this film as consultant, *no!* For your time consumed, you're entitled to the fee. Give it to Rabbi Heber's day school, he got you into this thing in the first place. Or keep the fee. What you give away you haven't got. As usual, you'll do as you please. All right?"

"All right. Thanks."

"You're welcome. I have to feed Candy," and she's gone.

GRANIT PRODUCTIONS
10 CENTURY PLAZA
CENTURY CITY, CA 90067

Margolit Solovei
Hotel Catalina
Cottage 4
Avalon, CA 90704

Margo—
    Do you know how radiant you looked coming out of the Falcon? Not a trace of fatigue, transfigured by triumph! You looked twenty years old. We all talked about it. You're dead right to hole up for a week and catch your breath, but let me at least send you the Production Book. It's a tome. If you like, Bronko can fly out and discuss the Book. I've never had a production manager to equal him, he's like an army chief of staff. Dearest Margo, all my old-fogey pique at you was stupid. Wouk won't turn down your marvelous script. It's *Zuleika* days again, only on a grand scale. We'll have a blast, you and I, and put Cecil B. DeMille in the shade!

Love,
Arnie

P.S. You know, you never did explain why Aaron and Moses were punished for Rock II, as you promised! Just curious.   A.

Herman Wouk

Mr. Louis Gluck
Gluck Metals
Melbourne—Houston

Dear Mr. Gluck:

I have read Margolit Solovei's screenplay, *The Lawgiver.* It is a workmanlike job, faithful to the subject matter. As I told you at the outset, the art of film is not my forte, but so far as my judgment matters, I approve the screenplay for production.

Since I was not consulted in the writing, nor will I be during the production, my name will not appear on the screen. For the time I did put in, Mrs. Wouk will negotiate a fee which will go to Rabbi Heber's local day school. He arranged our first meeting through Mr. Jacobs, you may remember.

My wife and I hope the film will be a box office success, rewarding you as backer and Mr. Warshaw as producer.

Sincerely,

Herman Wouk

cc: Timothy Warshaw

From: Louis Gluck
To: Herman Wouk
Subject: Solovei screenplay

Mr. Wouk:

At your wife's curry party I talked to Pearl Nightingale for ten minutes and was sure she could do the job, providing she had to earn your approval. I will proceed with WarshaWorks. My respects to your wife. She is a great woman, and that is why you are a great author.

Ad maya v'esrim,[1]

Louis Gluck

---

1. Hebrew. Literally, *"To a hundred and twenty"* (the age of Moses). "Best wishes" to one my age.—HW

From: Louis Gluck
To: Hezzie Jacobs
Subject: Lawgiver loans,
                Nullarbor investment

Smodar is sending you the balance due on your loans to WarshaWorks, plus interest. It is a lot of money. I will match you dollar for dollar on the new investment you propose for the extraction system at Nullarbor Ponds. Avoid those movie *drayers* hereafter, Hezzie, you were a fool, just lucky this time.

Louis Gluck

Louie,

Movie investments and root canal jobs have too much in common. Never again. Dr. Gillespie laughed and cried at the news of your go-ahead for the extraction system! A thousand thanks!

Hezzie

WARSHAW: Shayna? Are you there?

DANIELS: For heaven's sake, Tim, you and your two a.m. calls!

WARSHAW: Sorry, sorry, this won't take long. Guess what, Shayna? Gluck is in.

DANIELS: He *is?* Bless the Lord, O my soul!

WARSHAW: Amen. Skin of our teeth. You're the first to know. Cancel all arrangements to freeze *Aeneas*. Go ahead full steam; you have your budget. So has Arnie Granit. Looks like two big ones coming down the pike, partner, for the summer of 2014!

DANIELS: Perry Pines set, then?

WARSHAW: Not a problem, question of money, that's all. Amazing media interest just goes on and on—

DANIELS: So. No more Mr. Penis . . .

WARSHAW: No more, on your life! It's *Moishe Rabenu*, hear? Go back to bed, pleasant dreams. Now I call the bank.

Arnie!

I'm mad about Bronko! He just left on the helo. We got through the entire production book. I made a *ton* of notes. He says he's got the whole film in his head, shot by shot, and I believe him. Turns out his father was a Holocaust survivor, and he's passionate about this project, sort of like old Mr. Gluck. Let's meet, the three of us, first thing Monday and hit the ground running.

And thanks for your sweet note about how I looked coming off the Falcon. Fact is, I checked in the restroom mirror an hour out. Horrors. Death warmed over. I spent the hour working on my battered self, maybe that helped. And scrub that old-fogey stuff, Arnie dear, you know better. Remember the night out here when we got the giggles over Perry's "cold wet nose," and talked about your wife? That's our bond. Once a year my father dances with the Torah, and that was my mood almost straight through the job, thanks to you. When I had lapses into despair at my inadequacy, I told myself, "Arnie is waiting for more pages," and I *wrote*.

See you Monday.

Love,

Margo

Margo, my dearest,

Read, God yes! Burn, not yet. Not yet! I keep reading your Ayers Rock letter over and over. You'll never write another letter like that. You'll never have another such night. Few people know such joy in a whole lifetime. Those hours will weigh against whatever happens in the rest of your life, *ad maya v'esrim* (if you remember, you far-drifted rebel).

A drop to the mundane. Kiamesha Lake, ever heard of it? Formerly the heart of the Borscht Belt, it's now a Hasidic enclave. Cy's parents run a little family hotel there, Kiamesha Lodge. His grandparents started it long before the Borscht Belt erupted all over the Catskill Mountains, then died off, and the Hasidim came. The lodge survives, a quaint relic of forgotten days, hidden among tall pines and oaks, and still open for business. Early on Cy brought me there to meet his folks, and in fact he proposed to me out on the lake, in the lodge's one leaky rowboat. Gorgeous sunset over autumn trees, unsteady kisses in a rocking boat, and wet feet, such was our betrothal! Cy loves Kiamesha, grew up there, and we'll be married there. Just family, Cy and I decided on that last Sunday when I visited him. I suspect my parents will be relieved. I know I will be. A New York Jewish wedding is a pricey whoop-de-do, especially for a father of the bride who's a Hebrew school principal. So, dear, no maid of honor, no schlep for you across America and into the Catskills. You're off the hook.

Now then. If you're standing, sit down, if you're sitting, hang on to your chair. From the hospital I went to Maxim's and ordered up a steak, with bourbon on the rocks to calm my beating heart. Marrying in Kiamesha! The die is cast! My mind drifts back to that autumn sunset, the rocky rowboat, the wet feet, I'm in a sweet reverie when who walks in but AVRAM SCHARF, *with Shirley clinging to his arm like a new bride,* both of them in a lovey-dovey glow! They see me and greet me with small grins as they pass my table. Not a trace, not a *ghost,* of embarrassment, either one. I'm almost too dumbfounded to eat. There they sit, joking with the waiter as he takes their orders. Shirley catches my eye, gives me a bright smile, and twiddles her fingers. Soon she comes over and plops down in my booth. "Hearty appetite!" she says. "Know what? We're going to the Galápagos!! Second honeymoon, on a kosher windjammer! How about that?"

"*Kosher* windjammer?" I blurt.

"Oh, it's the newest thing. Cruise ships are so boring, aren't they, and so crowded! Eat, eat, eat! Well, there are these beautiful tall sailing ships, and now this special one, the *Moby Dick*, with an all-kosher cuisine. Rabbi Hoffenstein sailed on the *Moby Dick* last year, and couldn't praise it enough, especially the sautéed flying fish. It was a question whether flying fish were kosher, so he checked by texting Rabbi Krantz in Caracas. They're okay! Say, how's Cy? So nice to see you. Regards to Margo, if you keep in touch. Has her movie died? I just read some foolishness about an Australian nobody playing Moses. Crazy! Well, nice to see you."

Solid gold truth, Margo! I shouldn't be running on like this, but we do share a guilty taste for roast Shirley. Whether it's kosher, I may text Rabbi Hoffenstein.

One more thing, love. In your night at the Rock, did the Book of Ruth ever cross your mind?

Love,

Debbie

Dearest Debbie:

Your keen Bais Yaakov brain *would* zero in like a guided missile on the Book of Ruth.

Okay, keep the letter another day or two, then burn it, on your honor! I rolled around laughing at Shirley and the windjammer. Kiamesha—even the name—sounds like paradise lost. I envy your waterborne betrothal, wet feet and all. So different from my own state! Neither maid, wife, divorced, widowed, betrothed, *nothing,* just deliriously happy when I think about it. That's mostly when I wake up or go to bed. Otherwise all is the roar of a giant film under way: models of sets, costume designs, storyboard arguments, casting, a new Arnold Granit epic charging ahead full steam.

About the Book of Ruth, of course I thought of it. The two Bible books I know like the back of my hand are the Song of Songs and Ruth. Not for any pious reason. On the contrary! When I was about twelve, my hormones started percolating, curiosity about sex was getting to me, and those two books were my secret hot reading. The public library was forbidden. I *lived* Ruth in my daydreams, especially that passage about her crawling under Boaz's blanket, while the intense poetic pictures in the Song of Songs plagued me with frustrated longings. Very early on Tatti explained to me—on Pesach, I guess, when the Song of Songs is read in the synagogue—that it's all an allegory for the love between God and the Jewish people. Right, *right,* I thought! HA! My present "rebellion," as you choose to put it, was seeded then and there. Mind you, I was then the most religious girl in Bais Yaakov, sleeves down to here, skirt down to there, Tatti's pride and joy, doing spectacular memory feats in the Torah, even as X-rated phantom delights were bedeviling my soul.

But if the blanket scene is your clue to my night at Uluru, your guided missile splashes. The parallel goes deeper. Out of all the fields in the Bethlehem wheat harvest, the poor Moabitess convert, destined to be King David's great-grandmother, all unknowingly gleans in the field of a rich relative, Boaz. How come?

"*Vayikra mikreh*," says the Bible, two difficult Hebrew words. As a teenager I ransacked the public library for translations. A modern Jewish Bible gave "*as luck would have it,*" not bad but rather flat. Most versions are longer and clumsier. The best by far is still King James: "*her hap was to light on . . .*" Her HAP! What a clear strong Anglo-Saxon monosyllable! Well, my *hap,* against astronomic odds, was to fly to Australia on a film project and light at Ayers Rock in Josh Lewin's tent. Chance? Destiny? *Vayikra mikrehah . . .*!

I do have a few second thoughts—thoughts that I can tell only you. I wrote you what my father said when I moved out at seventeen, remember? Ah, Debbie, even by his lights I almost made it, didn't I? But that was *only* because no guy was Joshua, no other reason. In great confidence, I did have one pretty close call with the Broadway composer Biff Getz (*Savonarola: The Musical*) when I was filming *Barnard Blues* in New York. We met at Sardi's, became a twosome for lunch and late supper, all very much on the up-and-up. Not prepossessing, Biff, but lots of fun. Safe, you know? Yet I was beginning to like him a lot, and he sensed it. We went to a musical opening together, came out arguing about the show, and went on arguing into his SoHo flat, first time for me. A cozy pad, framed posters of his hit shows and the like. The Chardonnay flowed freely, the dispute continued warmly, and all at once, flashing a wicked Savonarola grin, Biff outs with, *"Let's go to bed."* Just like that. No pass, no foreplay. Shock and awe! No doubt this put many a suggestible gal flat on her back in that pad. I responded, cool as a Popsicle, "Thanks, Biff, but no." My! How my pudgy little Savonarola did wilt, and pout, and sulk, and berate me! I'm almost out the door when he hurls a last poisoned zinger, *"Good riddance, Marjorie Morningstar!"* Little did he know.

So anyway, right now I'd have some trouble looking Tatti in the eye. Not guilt, not a bit of it! Strong conditioned reflex, nothing else. A few months from now it won't matter—Shucks, my cell phone's acting up like mad, Arnie Granit's *Xenophon* theme. More very soon. *No* Robert Louis Stevenson this time, I promise. Just what happens next!

Love,

Margo (not quite Marjorie)

Chapter Eleven

TATTI

Margo: Arnie, what's up?

Granit: Is your father's name Moishe Solovei?

Margo: Why do you ask?

Granit: He's here.

Margo: Here? *Where,* here?

Granit: Here in my office. Tall man all in black, big black hat, graying beard? *(Silence.)* Want to talk to him? *(Very long silence.)* Margo, he's carrying a *Lawgiver* script.

Margo: *WHAT?*

Granit: That's why George brought him in to me. George says the studio gate cop mistook him for an extra. Green binder, runs up to page seventy-seven, third draft, middle of Spy sequence. It's for real, Margo, however he got it—*(Noises off.)* He asks to talk to you.

275

Margo: Oh, no, no, wait, not on the phone!
(Pause.) Oh, God, oh God, better
bring him here, Arnie.
Granit: To Catalina?
Margo: Yes, yes, give me a chance to
think! Oh, God—
Granit: *(Noises off.)* Okay, we're coming.

From: Deborah Kamaiko
To: Margolit Solovei

Dear,

Forgive me if I nag, but I have a very lousy feeling about what's happening with you. Mental telepathy? I keep checking and checking my e-mails and my fax machine. If you're okay, I can wait another day. (Barely!) No matter what, I'm *not* intruding with a phone call.

Debbie

Debbie—

Thanks, love, for not intruding. The mental telepathy is spot-on. I'm waiting in fear and trembling for a call from Josh, he's meeting right this minute with my father in Passaic! I can start to fill you in on what's been happening with me, but when he rings I must break off. To start with, Arnold Granit was calling me yesterday to tell me my father was there in his office! Fell in on him like a thunderbolt, *holding a copy of my incomplete screenplay.* Can you picture my shock, my stupefaction? Not to keep you in the suspense that racked me for hours, the explanation was simple and dull. My brother, Beshie, had sent the script to him.

[Margo recapitulates what happened. When she took Beshie's newlywed bride for a barefoot walk on the Catalina beach, Beshie peeked into the pile of draft scripts on her desk and decided to filch one for his father to read. Predictably, Tatti slung it away on a low bookshelf without a glance, but their mother, cleaning the office, came on it and insisted that he read it.]

278

. . . So Arnie went off to the hotel bar, and there stood my father in my Catalina hideout, a dour black-clad presence not much changed. Seeing him in the flesh touched off in me strong teenage reflexes of love and fear. We spoke only Yiddish, in a *scène à faire* straight out of old-time Yiddish theater, the stern religious father confronting his strayed repentant daughter, except that I wasn't repentant, just discombobulated and, at first, plain scared. When he started to discuss my screenplay in his old pedantic way of teaching Torah, the rebellious artist **MARGO** kicked in, bristling for a fight, but my combativeness gradually yielded to surprise, incredulity, and then relief and gratitude. Tatti liked what I had done. Ran through it all, liked it all! He began by calling my Genesis prologue an *einfal*, an inspiration, and ended by saying that my Moses on Mt. Nebo was the *Moishe Rabenu* he had taught me. He summed up, "In short, Mashie, my daughter, about moving pictures I know nothing, but I see you are doing a Kiddush Hashem, and I have come to tell you this, face-to-face."[1]

---

1. Kiddush Hashem: "Sanctification of the Name," the highest term of praise in the Jewish faith.—HW

With that, Debbie, the scene peaked in living heartrending Yiddish theater, lachrymose breakdown and all. I burst into tears. I threw myself into his outstretched arms. He soothed me in cooing Yiddish, and oh, friend of my bosom—

Christ, there's Josh—

Mashie

From: Deborah Kamaiko
To: Margolit Solovei
Subject: My Wedding Date

Mashie,

What a scene! What a terrific relief to hear from you! Cy gets discharged from the hospital next week, something we found out only two days ago. The date is still up in the air. Nothing Jewish is simple. Cy says there's a stonewalling impasse in Kiamesha, *which rabbi?* The two front-runners are the Sullivan County senior old-timer in Monticello and a Hasidic upstart. The hotel clientele is divided in loyalty between the two holy men, and hell will freeze over before they'll officiate together. This may have to go up to the UN Security Council.

Now, *what* transpired between Josh and your father that makes you ask about my wedding?

Debbie

MARGOLIT SOLOVEI
10321 MELROSE AVENUE
BEVERLY HILLS, CA 94721

Debbie, dear,

I've ducked out to my Melrose flat in the lunch break from an all-day conference in Granit's office. Filming on location starts next week—river north of Sacramento, marvelous stand of reeds, Pharaoh's daughter finds baby Moses, all mighty exciting.

Now, brief bald update on Josh and my father. When I whispered to Tatti that I'd been "as man and wife" with him, he let me say no more. A growl, *"Him? Him? Ach, that mamzer,*[2] where is he? Let me talk to him!" I got Josh at his office on my bedroom phone. Tatti sent me out and closed the door. I could hear harsh, muffled talk until Arnie came to warn me Tatti was booked

---

2. *Mamzer:* in Bible Hebrew, the child of an incestuous union; in Yiddish, loosely, a bastard.

to fly back to Newark soon. I made bold to enter the bedroom. Tatti hung up and forthwith left with a grave, chill good-bye, not another word. Of course I rang Josh at once. "Well, he called me a *mamzer*. Tell you more tonight," Josh said, "a big client is waiting very patiently in the outer office—"

"Josh, he called you that to me. *Bottom line,* for heaven's sake?"

"Well, now, my darling, that's a question of Yiddish nuance." He lapsed into his judicious lawyerly drawl: "*Mamzer* with angry tone and fierce scowl, a vile no-good. *Mamzer* with rueful headshake and wry smile, a clever scamp . . . not that easy to sort out over the phone—"

"Come on, you devil, you talked for twenty minutes—"

"Mostly what you'd call halakhic abracadabra.[3] Love you. Call you at nine tonight your time, tell you all. 'Bye."

He did call last night, reported his talk with Tatti, and *listen,* Debbie, I have a

---

3. Halakhah: "the way," Jewish religious law—legalistic mumbo jumbo.

brainstorm, woke with it in the wee hours, never went back to sleep. Tatti's first barked words when Josh came into his study were *"Mi darf gleich shtellen a chuppah!"*[4] No need to translate, eh, puss? Now here's the brainstorm, and your stonewalling rabbis fit in like a missing jigsaw piece. I cadge a WarshaWorks Falcon, pick up my parents at Newark Airport, and we fly to an airfield near Kiamesha for a double wedding ceremony! Cover story: you and I want it, the guys will do it, my film schedule compels a rush-rush ceremony, in and out over-night, and—*Tatti officiates!*

Hey, it's quarter past one. Granit must be having a fit over at the conference. What say about my brainstorm?

M.

---

4. "We must at once put up a canopy": Yiddish shorthand for a marriage with shotgun overtones.—HW

From: Deborah Kamaiko
To: Margolit Solovei
CC: Joshua Lewin
Subject: Double wedding

Dear Sleepless Brain—

Brilliant. BRILLIANT! I talked to Cy's mother (she runs the lodge, his dad is bookkeeper and handyman) and she'd love to finesse the stone-walling rabbis. I can deliver the lodge, you deliver Tatti, and it's a done deal! Date will depend entirely on your filming schedule, Cy will be recuperating at the lodge, and if it's anytime soon he'll be leaning on a crutch or cane. Kiamesha Lake is ringed with airports since Borscht Belt days, a good one is Sullivan International outside Monticello, figure a 45-minute limo run to the lodge.

We once corresponded about your being my maid of honor, remember? This is a *million* times sweeter. At long last we'll *see* each other, under a canopy—both as honest women!

Hot dog!

Debbie

From: Joshua Lewin
To: Margolit Solovei
Subject: Brainstorm, etc.

Hi, Mashie—

Off to Australia with Sheldon Rubinstein in a few hours via LAX. He's our entertainment man, aggressive smart negotiator.

Double wedding at Kiamesha? Glorious idea! Cy agrees. No problem for me, I drive up with my folks, but are you sure you've thought it through? Your brainstorm turns on bringing Tatti to officiate. That means four days of the company Falcon. Do you have that much clout? You've probably forgotten the Sabbath travel problem I live with. Tatti leaves Sunday and must return by Thursday: one day to Kiamesha, two days for nuptials, one day back to Passaic, one extra day to cover weather problems. Bad storm and he's stuck in an airport on *Friday, oy vey!* What to eat, where to sleep, just picture it! Tell Tatti what's involved, that's all. To nail me down he'll take steep risks.

About tonight, the idiot travel agent booked Sheldon and me into a double room. It's only for a few hours, our morning flight leaves very early, but Uluru seems a decade ago, and I'm absolutely dying to see you. Let's meet for a drink, and count now on our spending time together when I return, all you can spare from filming, okay? I'll erase my calendar for that.

See you tonight, girl of my long lonely dreams?

Josh

From: Margolit Solovei
To: Joshua Lewin

All right, dear. So about our chaste reunion tonight: what hotel, which bar, and what time? Let me know, and I'll be there. Now, when exactly will you be back for the "time we will spend together"? I guess we settle that over the drink? You seem to have figured out a lot of objections to my brainstorm. Well, things may change fast in the film business, but I do have the clout now. And yes, it's been quite a while since the Shabbat travel problem mattered to me. I guess I'd better get used to it again. You're right about Tatti, he'll take any risk, and believe it only when he sees with his own eyes that you slide the ring on my finger. Old Jewish wisdom.

Oh, room number of you and Sheldon? Just in case I have to check if you're late —or something.

Margo

Debbie, old thing,

> *God's in His heaven—*
> *All's right with the world . . .*

There's no snobbery in quoting Browning to a lit prof. That's my mood, and it would be yours too had you just breakfasted in bed at high noon in a glittery new hotel on a Dover sole at $85 and Blue Mountain coffee at about $10 a sip, tab all paid for. News flash, our double wedding is on! Josh is in, and Tatti somewhat grimly consents. I asked Arnie Granit about breaks in the production schedule, and he'll furnish me dates when I can be spared for four days.

Now about the Dover sole, just in case you're wondering.

Yesterday I texted Josh a sharp-clawed note worthy of Shirley Scharf. I was—not to put too fine a point on it—mighty pissed off at him. He was en route to Australia, overnighting at LAX. Unromantic, utterly businesslike, he texted me to meet him at his hotel for a late drink. Do you ever wish, after you've hit Send, that a siren had sounded and these words flashed: ARE YOU POSITIVE, IDIOT? I had an instant sinking feeling that my bitchiness was a horrible mistake. He came right back with short kind words which sort of reassured me. So I went to the appointed bar at the appointed time. No Josh. Five minutes, ten minutes. No Josh. *Too bitchy, I knew it! I'm getting the freeze. I deserve it. . . .* A smooth concierge, an Asian, approaches me. "Are you by chance Margo, madam?" Message on a plate: *Margo, come up to Room 2012,* though he had texted me Room 507. Elevator shoots me to the top floor. Josh opens the door on a plush room with floor-to-ceiling windows, vast view, movable bar, the works—

"Good Lord, Josh, what's this? And where's Sheldon?"

"Sheldon's down in 507. I don't know what I could have been thinking, love, just a drink in a bar." He twines his fingers in mine, leads me to another door, throws it open on a great round red-covered bed in a sizable room stacked around with roses. "Bridal suite."

I was struck dumb, hit on the head—shoot, there's room service with my Blue Mountain refill—*got* to get going! I promised Arnie a rewrite on Pharaoh's daughter today. Can't do it on my iPhone, sitting up in bed. Quickly then, over the coffee: the concierge had set this up, of course. The bridal suite is usually on tap at a price, and these Asian hotel types, so Josh says, look you in the eye and know your net worth. Loosened up by a scotch on the rocks—it wasn't a Champagne moment at *all*, Deb, you'll understand that—I asked him something that's been plaguing me. Exactly what had he told Tatti about Uluru? What had gone on in that long Catalina phone talk and the face-off in Passaic?

Well, I found out. Tatti's love, his raison d'être, is the Talmud, he learns it day and night. Josh knows a lot from YU days, but he's no match for Tatti, not a prayer. He ventured to cite a Talmud passage: *A woman is acquired by money (today, a ring), document (marriage contract), and intercourse (just what it means).*[5] On that third option, Tatti hit him with a barrage of

---

5. Tractate Kiddushin (Marriages). Chapter 1, Paragraph 1.—HW

qualifying Bible exegesis and Talmud authorities. Josh fought back, which practically endeared him to Tatti, who reveled in crushing him. That consumed the time.

"Are you telling me," I said, draining my second scotch, "that when you muttered a little Hebrew in that bed, you thought you were marrying me?"

"Well, no, but there you were, sweetie pie, in my arms under my blanket, weren't you? It showed intent, at least."

"In short, halakhic abracadabra." I got up and walked to the window. "Amazing view. What time is your plane?"

I'm clasped from behind. I get spun around and kissed, kissed again and again. As soon as I can breathe I gasp, "I asked, *when* is your plane?"

He says, "Okay, okay. Once a brazen wench, always a brazen wench." He leads me to that other door, opens it on roses, roses, roses . . .

CAMERA: Holds on closing door. Very slow FADE TO BLACK.

ORCHESTRA: (sneaks in) Lohengrin's "Wedding March."

CAMERA: Still holding on door. Very slow FADE IN, dawn brightening on the door.

ORCHESTRA: Modulates to Jewish wedding dance music. Chorus of many joyous voices, young, old, "Mazel tov," "Hava Nagila," stamping of dancing feet . . . music on and on, through the credits . . .

There appears in huge, slightly Hebraic letters

THE END

Once a screenwriter, always a screenwriter, beloved Debbie. See you under the canopy!

Forever yours,

Margo
A.K.A. the brazen wench

EPILOGUE

From *Moby-Dick*, the last page:
The drama's done. Why then here does any one step forth?

From *The Will to Live On*:
The Lawgiver *remains unwritten. I have never found the way to do it.*

Just a word, gentle reader, about how I found a way to do it.

In April 2009, a month short of my ninety-fourth birthday, I submitted to my publisher a slender typescript on which I had labored long years.[1] Reasonably wild with enthusiasm, he scheduled it for publication in a year. I was used to having my novels rushed hot to the press, but this was a meditation on faith and science, no doubt judged unlikely to fly off Barnes & Noble's shelves. All the same, I was graveled. A whole year, at my age! Intolerable wait! Would I even be around when the book saw the light?

---

1. *The Language God Talks* (New York: Little, Brown, 2010).

Well, I decided, let's have a go at another novel, if only to pass the time. But what novel? I hadn't the ghost of an idea for one. For years, indeed decades, there had been a standing joke in my family about an *"impossible novel"* I wanted to write but would never discuss. Unknown to them a scuffed file lay in my desk labeled *The Lawgiver*; it contained "a few typed yellow pages turning brown with age." Now, having nothing to do but kill a year, I girded up my loins, in scriptural parlance, and wrote a few Moses scenes. I started at the Burning Bush, worked hard, reread the scenes, and there lay the prose. Limp, lifeless. I sank into despair, hit bottom hard, and the bolt of lightning struck: WRITE A LIGHTHEARTED NOVEL ABOUT THE IMPOSSIBILITY OF WRITING A NOVEL ABOUT MOSES. In the dazzle of that flash, Louie Gluck came rolling into my office, hard upon it Margo wrote her chilly Rosh Hashanah letter to poor faithful Joshua, and I had my star-crossed lovers who would uncross their stars in the tent at Ayers Rock. The producers Tim Warshaw and Shayna Daniels were already on hand from my last novel.[2] Debbie, Hezzie, Perry Pines, Adin, Smallweed, Cy, Hviesten, and the rest all waited in the wings, and entered the tale on cue. Shirley Scharf elbowed herself in, an irrelevant irritant,

2. *A Hole in Texas* (New York: Little, Brown, 2004.

but on instinct I let her stay. After a while the love troubles of Shirley, Avram, and Hviesten, intersecting the love troubles of Debbie and Cy, did mesh pretty well, and the Scharfs' second honeymoon on the *Moby Dick* was the clincher. You never know, in the narrative art.

With the closing of the door to the bridal suite, my players were gone. The play was played out, and Margo, with her story savvy, faded to black and brought up the wedding music. Yet what of the *Lawgiver* movie—how did it turn out? And what of these people I had called into being and grown fond of? The nineteenth-century novelists (I've been called the last of them) were wont to end their tales with a sizable time lapse and a brief rounding out of the characters' later lives. Trouble is, I am myself a main character in *The Lawgiver* (the novel), writing in real time right now in October 2011. When old Gluck rolled into my office, he nailed me and BSW into the story once and for all. Thus I can offer only my own light-hearted surmise about the future of the movie and of my characters. Truly your guess is as good as mine, friend reader, about what happened next.

But about BSW, my last word will be in real time.

Daily Variety headlined its box office report on *Aeneas and Dido* and *The Lawgiver*, released simultaneously nationwide by WarshaWorks in the dead of summer.

WARSHAW'S DOUBLE WHAMMY!

" 'Boffo' doesn't begin to hack it," the report began. "All Hollywood assumptions about summer releases are exploded. Executives are in shock. Power agents reel." So it went on in stammering showbiz jargon about the astounding grosses of both epic films.

On *Time*'s cover, Perry Pines as Moses and as Achilles stand side by side:

WARSHAW'S AUDACIOUS GAMBLE

The cover story inside shows Warshaw in shirtsleeves at his desk. The protean film plunger smiles at a sheaf of box office reports with (as Mark Twain put it) the calm confidence of a Christian with four aces. "Conventional wisdom is a slippery slope to flops," he pontificated to *Time*. "My decision was strictly seat-of-the-pants. The audience of Pines as Achilles is feeding the audience of Pines as Moses, and vice versa. It started big, it will stay big."

Inspired folly? Amazing smarts? Either way, as the industry gasps at his coup, the stock of

WarshaWorks is rocketing, while Perry Pines, the newly anointed box office king from Down Under, ignores the frantic flood of raves and pans from Up Over. Sequestered on the huge sheep farm which he bought with his fee for playing Moses after superstars all passed, he says his resolve to return to sheep farming for good, unavailable to the media and all film offers, seems ironclad. Warshaw remains breezily skeptical. "I know human nature pretty well," he says, "and actors' natures very well. Give Perry Pines five years and a great script, and he'll be back before the cameras."

Margo Solovei isn't so sure. The writer-director who, with veteran producer Arnold Granit, created the biblical smash hit suspects that Pines will remain among his sheep. Interviewed by *Time* in her Catalina cottage retreat, where reviews and box office reports littered her desk, she pointed with pride at an article in *The New York Review of Books* by Shaya Krimski, headed "The Phenomenology of Moviegoing." Citing Schopenhauer's strictures in his *Parerga and Paralipomena* on Hegel's iconic triads, Krimski discerns in the gory Achilles (thesis), the godly Moses (antithesis), and the reclusive Australian Perry Pines playing both roles a naive numinous synthesis. "*There's* perception, *there's* recognition," she exults. "And that's Perry."

• • •

Just a surmise, that. Now for my other characters. Shirley and Avram Scharf lived happily ever after, except for a prolonged paternity lawsuit brought by Else Hviesten against Avram, asserting he had fathered her twin daughters. The tots were three years old before the matter was amicably resolved, when a move to extradite Avram was making some headway in the State Department. Junkyard Dog Janeway flew to Norway with a medically certified sample of Scharf's DNA and a modest settlement offer. Her lawyers pooh-poohed the DNA and jumped at the settlement.

Some time after the Perry Pines box office sensation, James Bearing received a startling letter from Australia. He complied with the instructions therein and replied, *"Dear Mr. Pines: As per your letter and enclosure, I have conveyed the bank draft for US $25,000 to Mr. Geoffrey Smallweed, who was hard to track down, and I gave him your verbal message, 'You're forgiven.' I have no receipt, for he snatched the draft, capered around my office, and rushed out, leaving no address. Congratulations on your two successful films, and on retiring while you were ahead. Very truly yours, etc."*

Perry Pines married Sally Robertson shortly before he acquired the farm. She had just turned

299

sixteen, and he had been waiting for her to grow up since she was five. He exhibits no interest whatever in returning before Warshaw's or anyone else's cameras.

Adin Genakowski shared the Nobel Prize in Genetics with a scientist from Finland. Margo wrote him a note of congratulations on a personal card and forgot about it. Some months later a three-page letter came from him about religion, Israel, and his new wife, of such an intensely personal nature that she never showed it to Josh. But she kept it. Genakowski is married to Hepzibah Zivoni.

Not long ago, Hezzie Jacobs sent me a first-edition copy of *Marjorie Morningstar*, asking me to sign it as his wife Rachel's bat mitzvah gift to their daughter Harmonie. "We think at her age Harmonie can handle it," he explained. Apparently in some circles that gentle book is still classed with the Kama Sutra. Louie Gluck is not only very much alive, Hezzie reports, he has had the cockpit of his Gulfstream reconfigured with hand controls at the copilot seat and is taking flying lessons. Their algae venture is going strong. Their green gasoline now figures at $700 a gallon, gradually if slowly dropping.

Thomas Peacock: Love and Age in India House, a much praised scholarly work and a surprise modest best seller, brought Professor Deborah Kamaiko-Diamond of New York University invitations to join the English departments of both Princeton and Georgetown. Since Cy was serving in the Pentagon as a career personnel officer, she chose Georgetown. They settled down in McLean and as yet have no children. Debbie writes rueful letters to Margo about that. "We both have been tested and retested fertile by one damned gynecologist after another. One of them giggled, 'Just luck of the throw.' We keep throwing. Fun, if a shade dismal."

* * *

So much and no more for surmise. Margo's "Fade to black" was convincing and final. What will happen to my lovers beyond that dark veil even I cannot guess. I did try. In my pass at their future, here is what I came up with.

The surprise success of *Musa*, the Arabic release of *The Lawgiver*, with subtitles—after all, Musa (Moses) is second only to the Prophet as a figure in the Koran—gave the high-riding Arnold Granit the notion of attempting *Hagar*, a spectacular movie about Sarah's handmaiden, the mother of Ishmael and the Arab nation. Margo dutifully went to work on a draft screenplay, until it turned out that she had become pregnant that night at Ayers Rock. A seismic shift took place in Margo's spirit. She had a rough time, a punishment of Eve right out of Genesis, twenty-three hours in labor.

When Josh had his first look at the infant, she said to him with a weary smile, "I want more of these," and the Hagar movie lapsed.

That is not so bad, maybe, but even as a lighthearted guess I can't believe a word of it.

* * *

Margo and Josh are blissfully yoked, that much I know. For all the troubles they inherit with their human nature, they will be one flesh, as in Genesis. Theirs is a marriage like mine with BSW, decades of happiness "ever after," for all the deep grief that was a vein of our fate together. Margo, like the others in my story, is a creature of imagination, but as I say in the novel, she much reminds me of the bittersweet girl I met by chance during a navy yard overhaul. With a couple of shipmates I crashed her birthday party on a Saturday night after the bars closed on Terminal Island. How can one get nearer to sheer chance? Or pure Providence? After two or three days we both knew that we would be one, though it was a long haul to 1945 and the war's end.

Betty Sarah Wouk, born Betty Carol Brown in Pelouse, Idaho, died very suddenly of a massive stroke, during the writing of this story, on March 17, 2011, here in our Palm Springs home. She was ninety. We shared our time under the sun for sixty-three years, during which I did all my literary work. Before we met I wrote nothing that mattered. Whoever reads a book by Herman Wouk will be reading art deeply infused with her self-effacing and incisive brilliance, books composed during a long literary career managed by her common sense, with which I am sparsely endowed.

Here is BSW, the girl I met by God's grace in 1944, a Phi Bete and an enchantment, working in Navy personnel. She rests in peace beside our firstborn son, who accidentally died in Mexico when almost five years old. My place at Abe's other side awaits me in God's good time. A few years ago I said to her I had three more books to write. "Is one of them fiction?" she inquired.

"Yes."

"Then write that one."

"Why?"

"Because we're living it up."

Her brand of Zen. Hence, *The Lawgiver.*

This is the small photograph mentioned in my book, which she sent me in a love letter to my ship at sea. It has been on my desk in all our wanderings. It will be there while I live to work on at the other two books.

Center Point Large Print
600 Brooks Road / PO Box 1
Thorndike ME 04986-0001 USA

(207) 568-3717

US & Canada:
1 800 929-9108
www.centerpointlargeprint.com